# EXTENSION–THIRD DIMENSION OF EDUCATION

# EXTENSION—THIRD DIMENSION OF EDUCATION

DR. G. PANKAJAM

GYAN PUBLISHING HOUSE
NEW DELHI-110002

Extension: Third Dimension of Education



ISBN: 9788121207096



Reprinted in 2015 in India by
Gyan Publishing House
5, Main Ansari Road, Daryaganj,
New Delhi - 110002
Phone : 23282060, 23261060
Fax : (011) 23285914
E-mail : books@gyanbooks.com
website: gyanbooks.com

# CONTENTS

# PREFACE

The educational institutions at all levels generate new knowledge and consider this as the prime task. The knowledge generated will become static and will stagnate at the portals of the universities and colleges, if we don't take the effort to disseminate it to the masses and make them use through extension programme. Hence, it is imperative that extension is an important vehicle to carry the fruits of teaching and research to the community. Education should aim at taking the results of research in the colleges and universities for field testing at the community level. The acceptance and use of the new knowledge alone will prove the worthiness of any research undertaken in the laboratories. The successes and failures of the knowledge at the field level should be ploughed back to further testing. This means every university and college should have an area of operation for field testing of any subject taught in the educational institutions. Both the student and the faculty should be made an integral part of the university curriculum.

Extension may also involve closer interaction with the society and could be dovetailed with the programmes of rural development. This should aim at inculcation of scientific temper and awareness of impact of several factors in day-to-day life—proper utilization of the fruit of science and technology, environment, education, legal literacy, national integration, etc. among the community around the university.

No educational institutions should be permitted to be isolated from the community so that education could be made more meaningful and need-based. If the educational institutions should be accountable to the society, they can survive. The accountability and commitment could be expressed through the extension programmes which every educated person could take up.

In a conference held in May, 1981, it was adopted that continuing and extension education should be an integral function of the universities and the colleges besides teaching and research. It was also emphasised that there should be greater co-ordination between extension activities, manpower planning, self-employment, social awareness and greater interaction with the local community. In 1984, it was also decided in the Vice-chancellors' conference that 'Adult and Continuing Education' should become an integral part of the university programme and should be institutionalised. Higher educational institutions involved in extension programme should aim at eradication of illiteracy, economic backwardness rise in population growth and poverty by permeating in all the disciplines of studies at all levels. The UGC in its policies frame of 1977 envisaged extension as an important third dimension of the higher education and emphasised that the university should absorb the concept of extension culture and efforts should be taken to allot 25 per cent time-period for the off campus, extension work through community education.

The UGC review committee set up under the Chairmanship of Dr Ramlal Parikh In 1986, had suggested extension activities to be undertaken by the institution of higher education such as universities and colleges and policy-making bodies like the Ministry of Human Resource Development, Government of India.

Thus, it becomes a necessity to all those who are involved in education at any level, to understand the need, principles, strategies and techniques of extension education, so that they could develop positive attitude for extension activities and acquire the skill in communication and techniques of extension education.

# 1

# INTRODUCTION

Education has three components, i.e. creating new knowledge through 'Research', disseminating it through 'teaching' and putting into practice or applying it through 'extension.' It means education cannot remain within four walls of the portals of educational institutions. It should relate itself to the community and its needs. Education cannot remain in isolation. Educational institutions should be owned by the community and should reflect the ideals, and needs of the community. All the resources available to the community and the educational institutions, should be shared by both. The local human resources available to the community should be tapped to strengthen the educational institutions. Similarly other resources of materials, intellectual capacity and potentialities of the teaching community should be utilized to empower the whole community. Intellectuals cannot remain inside the portals of educational institutions under the pretext that they belong to a different category and they could only preach not to practice. Unless every teacher knows and learns the art of innovation, discovery, effective communication and application, she/he will not be suitable for the teaching profession.

The concept of two different categories of people—those who think, the 'Think Tanks' great philosophers and those who could work only or implement what has been given by the thinkers—no longer could continue.One who thinks and not able to communicate means the knowledge remains stale, has no use to others. Thinking should become an instrument for action. Those who think and create new knowledge should come out to work for people by applying what they have invented.

Teachers should be able to identify the knowledge, that is useful to the society to solve their problems, increase the material resources and build up human resources. They should lead the students to take this useful knowledge to the community. This extension of useful information to those who need it, should be the ultimate aim of education which is the third dimension of education.

The process of extension or spreading the knowledge is through educating the farmers, housewives, women, or any village community, and not through compulsion or coercion or force. Education of rural people involves convincing them about the new knowledge so that they apply this knowledge in their fields or any situations to produce more or bring in change for better life.

The educational institutions at all levels generate new knowledge and consider this as the prime task. The knowledge generated will become static and will stagnate at portals of the universities, colleges, and schools if we do not take the effort to disseminate it to the masses and make them use through extension programme. Hence, it is imperative that extension is an important vehicle to carry the fruits of teaching and research to the community. Education should aim at taking the results of research in the schools, colleges and universities for field testing at the community level. The acceptance and use of the new knowledge alone will prove the worthiness of any research undertaken in the laboratories of the educational institutions. The successes and failures of the knowledge at the field level should be a feed back and ploughed back to, for further testing. This means every educational institutions, i.e. schools, university and every college should have an area of operation for field testing of any subject taught in the educational institutions. Extension components of education should become integral part of the curriculam, and for teachers and students to follow.

Extension may also involve closer interaction with the society and could be dovetailed with the programmes of rural development. This should aim at inculcation of scientific temper and awareness of impact of several factors in day-to-day life—proper utilisation of the fruit of science and technology, environment, education, legal literacy, national integration, etc., should be taken to the community around the educational institutions.

### *Concept of Extension*

According to D. Ensminger "Extension is education and its purpose is to change attitudes and practices of the people with whom the work is done". V.T. Krishnamachari says, "Extension is a continuous process, designed to make the rural people aware of their problems and indicating to them the ways and means by which they can solve them. It involves not only educating the rural people in determining their problems and methods of solving them, but also inspiring them towards positive action in doing so".

Extension is an out of school education process. It involves working with people along the lines of their current interest and need which are closely related to gaining livelihood, improving level of living, and catering the needs of community welfare; utilising particular teaching techniques, conducted with the aid of certain supporting activities and carried on with a distinctive spirit of co-operation, mutual respect, and help.

### *Objectives of Extension*

The essence of extension education is the adoption of changed practices by individuals based on their own decisions, leading to community or group action. The fundamental objective of extension, therefore, is to develop the individuals in the community and improve the well-being of all the rural people within the framework of national, economic, social and political policies and conditions.

Other objectives are, in the material side to increase production, in the educational side to increase knowledge, to improve strategies of teaching, skills and help people to change their attitudes from traditional and static to scientific and dynamic and in social and cultural sphere, to develop the community through consolidating and strengthening the local groups such as youth clubs, Mahila Mandals, Co-operatives, Panchayats, etc.

Extension is an educational process which seeks to bring about desirable changes in the behaviour not only of individual human beings but in the community as a whole. It is less formal and unstructured as compared to conventional, formal system of education. The concepts are derived not only from the field study and experience for the use of learners in the society through extension. Extension is an educational activity which tries to transmit knowledge, wisdom and skills to the community.

There is no need for a fixed curriculum in extension education. It is need-based, depending on the community. The learner can choose to learn. impart the knowledge according to his interest, capacity and community in which he lives. It needs not to be essential for the award of a certificate or degree. Extension is essentially an education procedure according to the needs of the community.

Extension education is mostly practical, field and problem oriented which may not lead to pure theoretical formulation. At the same time theoretical framework could also be envisaged through extension work. The problems faced and the success stories of extension work can lead to theory formulation as the guidance for future.

The users would comprise of schools, the pre-primary will depend on primary, the primary depends on the secondary, the secondary school depends of the higher education as each one contributes to the development of the other sector. Eventualy all these contribute to the development of the community and gets benefitted. Unless the educational institutions come closer to the community and involve themselves in the betterment of the community they cannot survive and the education provided by them will become futile.

Concepts to be extended through extension education need not to be confined to the classrooms. The whole community becomes the teaching and learning environment. There is no rigid teaching hours, and examination. With diversified goals, extension education is carried out in life situations, in the community.

### *Extension Education is Interdisciplinary*

Under extension education anything in life situations could be taught. It is interdisciplinary. Extension education includes concepts from various disciplines like law, science, management, home science, economics, agriculture, commerce, medicine, sociology, social work, technology, political sciences, environmental science, geography, etc.

Law students and the teachers could provide the legal literacy to the community by setting up legal aid cells and help the individuals, groups, and other social organisations in solving their problems.

The faculty and the students of management studies could help the workers as to how their skills could be enhanced, how to budget their time, etc. Trade union leaders, small entrepreneurs, businessmen, people having small-scale industries, researchers, social and cultural organisations could get guidelines from the department of management in the areas of setting up organisation, and management of their trade, business, industries and organisations.

Home science staff and the students could be of help in managing the homes by teaching the people in the community budgeting the money, time and energy. Efficient management of home, adjustment and child rearing could be taught to the young couple. They could spread the message of good nutritious food, health and sanitation and different roles that the family members have to perform. Women could be taught to supplement their family income through kitchen garden, poultry, handicrafts, etc.

Science students could help the community to develop scientific attitude, scientific temper and scientific approach to solve the problems of individuals as well as the society. Application of science in everyday life could be imparted, even to the illiterates, the farmers, housewives and others through small experiments and demonstrations.

Scientific concepts in technology whether high, medium or small-scale industries could be taken to the field and help the development of all these industries, in the communities around the educational institutions. By enhancing their skills of production we could produce more, earn more, and this helps the community to have an enriched happy life. Guiding the community to use the technical knowledge obtained in the classroom will solve the problem of poverty by producing more, in a scientific way.

Students and the staff of economics can help the community to plan for production, marketing and distribution. By having proper economic policy and planning, the community can expect an equitable distribution of commodities. Small and marginal farmers could also be helped to produce and market properly so that they earn what they are due to.

Students of medicine and schools of medicine can have definite roles in the society to improve its health and sanitation by providing healthcare services and teaching them the need for clean self or personal cleanliness and the environment. Preventive aspects could be taken up by the faculty by providing health education, preventive steps to be taken to control epedemics, as 'prevention is better than cure'. Health education can be introduced in school children so that good health habits are formed even during their formative years.

Colleges of education and Teacher Training Institutes could adopt the schools in their laboratory areas and provide all possible help and knowledge to improve the infrastructural facilities, teaching and learning atmosphere in the schools. In the nonformal system of education they could teach the dropouts, and child labours. By setting up child guidance cells in the community the young and the disturbed children, could be helped.

Sociology and social work faculty can study the structure and functions of the society, different social groups, the family system, their functions and other organisations. This would reveal the societal needs which would help them guide the society. Different needs and dimensions of the society require the modern concepts for better development.

Political science students can sensitise the community their power, roles, responsibilities and the rights, can create awareness among the voters on the need for voting and electing right type of leaders to vote them for power. Public can also be educated on different forms of governments, their merits and demerits or limitations and role of people in different forms of governments. Everybody in the community should be made aware of Panchayati Raj—the local government and the power and functions of people in it.

Environmental degradation and pollution have greater impact on individuals and the community. Hence the environmentalists and the scientists can create awareness on the importance of preserving the nature, disposal of waste material, to recycle it for further use and to undertake eco-friendly activities. Educate the mass to preserve the nature by planting trees and keeping the place clean.

Agriculture has got a wider scope in extension education as it could be of direct help to the farmers in villages, who constitute nearly 80 per cent of the Indian population. For the staff and students of agriculture courses farms will be the real laboratory. What they learn in the classroom could be tested on the land for its application. Whether it is of improved seeds, fertilizer, pesticides or improved methods of cultivation like use of machineries, etc. could be tested in the fields. Similarly consumption of agricultural products could be demonstrated to the community the village, or urban, educated or illiterates to be convinced by preparing various tasty dishes.

Global logo of development is sustainable development. Extension means promotion of learning avenues in the adjoining local communities which will be mutually interlinked with field programmes of all disciplines of study. Through extension, relevant knowledge, skills and values are transmitted to the community in a particular area. The area-based community approach is intended to make extension work specifically relevant to the people of all age groups of the adopted community.

Instead of taking a programme piecemeal to a community if we follow the area-based community approach it will help extension work relevant to all age groups and all disciplines. After identifying the needs of the different age groups if extension work is being planned it becomes more meaningful. This approach also makes the extension work participatory as people of all the age groups are involved and they help each other. This, in turn, will become peer group approach.

Extension work of all dimensions will lead to the total development of the community. It may be of adult education programme, awareness building programme, skill development programme, agricultural programme, women development programme, child care, supplementary programme, entrepreneurship programme, small-scale industries, health and nutrition hunger free programme, refresher courses of short duration, people education, etc. When all these inputs are taken to a specific area of the community all the age groups will be covered at the same time each will supplement and enrich the other.

Humanism in education and the development of community could be promoted or achieved only when educational institutions have link with the neighbouring communities. There should be a definite allocation and mobilisation of funds for this purpose. Lack of humanism and the link defeat the purpose of education and the learners are being taken away from the reality, and thus become alien in their own society.

Field work should become integral part of all subjects of study, whether it is science or humanity. The exposure to the community becomes need-based and the community also enriches and takes the responsibility of education than depending on any funding agency. Problem of unemployment and underemployment will be solved if we plan the education according to the human resources required.

We have to create in the minds of younger generation the desire to work and they must be exposed to different ideas, viewpoints, cultures, languages and traditions of helping the needy and poor in villages and the community around them. Youths should breakdown the barriers of sitting and learning within four walls and come out to work for others.

No educational institutions should be permitted to be isolated from the community so that education could be made more meaningful and need-based. All the educational institutions should be made accountable to the society, for their survival. The accountability and commitment could be expressed through the extension programmes which every institution and educated person could take up. Thus, through extension work a link between the Gown and the community is established.

In a conference held in May 1981, it was adopted that continuing and extension education should be an integral function of the universities and the colleges besides teaching and research. It was also emphasised that there should be greater co-ordination among extension activities, manpower planning, self-employment social awareness ano greater interaction with the iocal community. In 1984, it was also decided in the Vice-chancellors' conference that adult and continuing education should become an integral part of the university programme and should be institutionalised. Higher educational institutions involved in extension programme should aim at eradication of illiteracy, economic backwardness.

rise in population growth and poverty by permeating extension in all the disciplines of studies at all levels. The UGC in its policies frame of 1977 envisaged extension as an important third dimension of the higher education and emphasised that the university should absorb the concept of extension culture and efforts should be taken to allot 25 per cent time for the off campus, extension work through community education.

The UGC review committee set up under the chairmanship of Dr. Ramlal Parikh in 1986, had suggested extension activities to be undertaken by the institutions of higher education such as universities and colleges and policy-making bodies like the Ministry of Human Resource Development, Government of India.

Thus, it becomes a necessity to all those who are involved in education at any level, to understand the need, principles, strategies and techniques of extension education, so that they could develop positive attitude for extension activities and acquire the skill in communication and techniques of extension education.

### *Principles of Extension*

The following principles are to be kept in mind while taking up the extension work:

1. Extension is based on conditions that exist locally.
2. Extension work involves the people in actions that promote their welfare.
3. The extension worker does not assume leadership himself/ herself but works through local leaders.
4. Extension work should be voluntary and not compulsory.
5. There should be flexibility in extension programme.
6. Extension work is to be carried out in actual life situations.
7. Extension is both imparting and learning.
8. Education and Services are the two major components of extension, and
9. Extension work should be carried out from one's own experience and not merely on theoretical basis.

1. Each community should be considered as unique with its own problems, resources, characters, and needs. So, we must

understand the community first before we start the extension work to make the extension programme locale specific.

2. There can be no extension work unless the local people are involved willingly and participate actively in the extension programme, to promote their own welfare. The extension worker must work with the people and not for the people. Our motto of extension is to help the people to help themselves. Participatory approach in extension will lead to success.

3. The local leaders are to be identified and extension work is to be carried out through them, so that we could have people participation and accountability. Local leaders usually will be easily accepted by the people and the other local institutions like cooperatives, panchayats and educational institutions.

4. Extension work should be taken up by the individuals and the educational institutions voluntarily. Element of compulsion will eliminate the ultimate purpose of extension work.

5. It is essential to have flexibility in extension. Rigidity will spoil the freedom of the extension worker. The extension worker should be able to alter or change the programmes according to the situations so that the originality, creativity and innovations of the worker could be exhibited.

6. Extension work cannot be carried out in the classroom situations or in an artificially created atmosphere. Extension activities can be undertaken only in a real-life situation so that the results of the programmes could be applied in improving the community.

7. Extension is teaching as well as learning. By teaching new concepts to the community the extension worker learns whether they are really needed and accepted by the community. This feedback and learning help the worker to modify, change and adopt new strategies. So, extension is a two-way process of teaching and learning.

8. Education and services are the two sides of the same coin. There can be no extension education without service. Similarly services without education will not be of any permanent value. People should know the results of both these components.

9. Experience of any individual and the institutions should be the basis for extension work rather than mere theoretical

background; experience in the field would provide guidance and the alternative activities to be taken up in the extension programme.

The practices of rural people are tradition bound and not so easy to change their attitudes and practices. But the objective of extension is to bring about change in their knowledge, attitude and practices. The function of extension work therefore, is to provide learning situations whereby the people gain new knowledge, develop skills and attitudes necessary for adopting new and improved practices.

Learning takes place by seeing, hearing, touching, smelling and tasting. The extension method should include and appeal to all these senses so that learning becomes easy and retention is ensured. Only by adopting appropriate methods, the interest and the desire to learn new things could be evoked. The extension method should develop attention, interest, confidence action and satisfaction of the beneficiaries or the participants of the extension programme Fig. 1.1.

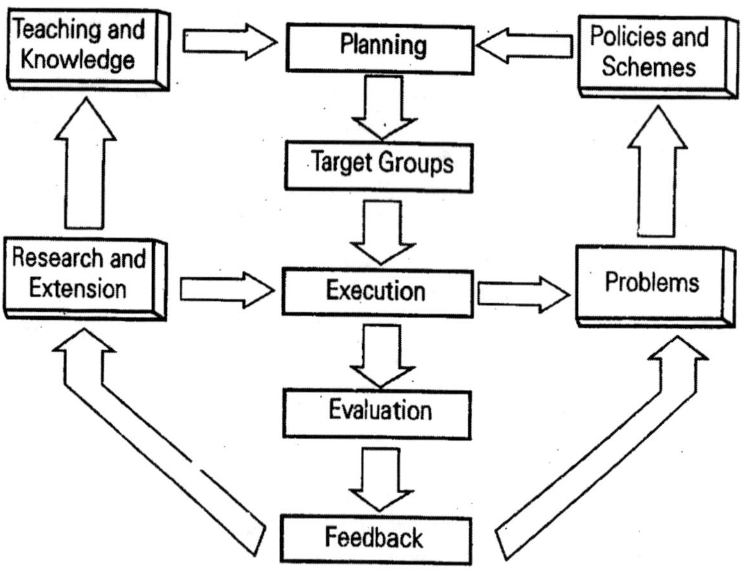


**Fig. 1.1: Extension Procedure.**

The following methods could be adopted in extension programmes:

1. Individual or personal contacts.
2. Demonstrations.
3. Meetings.
4. Study tours—field visits.
5. Campaigns.
6. Competitions.
7. Audiovisual aids like—charts, film strips, slide, posters, flannel graphs, flipbooks, exhibitions, puppets, movies and videos.

Educational institutions should become the 'brain banks' and the 'think tanks' and should be taught to utilise their thoughts for the betterment of the society. They should come forward to test their theory in the fields for their application. If all educational institutions and the students are encouraged, motivated and guided for taking the researches in the laboratory to the land the best form of extension education will emerge.

In the subsequent chapters in this book the readers will find required information that would help them to become efficient and committed extension workers and a desire for bringing about change among the people at their cognitive, affective and psychomotor domains. This change in attitude and skills of the academics will help build a new society which will be ready to face the challenges of the 21st century with confidence.

# 2

# HISTORICAL PERSPECTIVE

All nations desire to achieve progress and prosperity. Progress presupposes change in a chosen direction. Change, in turn, presupposes the creation or development of new knowledge and better technology on the one hand and its practical application on the other. In other words 'Education', 'Research' and Extension' are, sine qua non of progress in any field of national development.

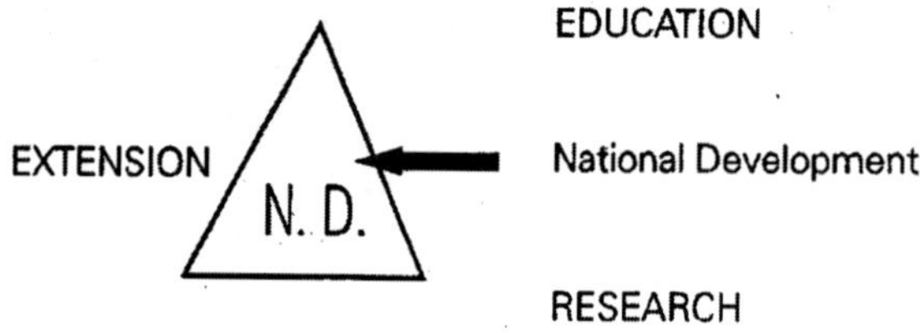


The role of 'extension worker' of today is quite different from that of his role in past. Extension education has now become a flexible type of education which serves the people wherever they are, whatever they are. The extension worker has, therefore, to adjust to the needs of the society and should know the varied facets of extension education.

***Need and Importance of Extension Education***

Extension work—the education of the people to help themselves—is thus selected as a means to bring out inevitable change in the right direction. Change is necessary to make the world a better place to live in. If change is judged to be both necessary and inevitable then the question arises:

Why Extension Education?

Men are not equipped with knowledge to make a proper choice. They may have a general desire for better living, but may not have a specific idea of what improvements are most desirable and feasible. They need to be taught true values. That is why "extension education" has been established.

Inventions are giving rise to new technology in every walk of life. Field of education is no exception to this phenomenon. Men find changes in teaching and learning process. These changes are to be taken to both learning and teaching community. The new strategies and technology in teaching and evaluation expect the teachers to have a new approach to teaching and evaluation.

The changes are also observed in the non-formal system of education. As there are children who drop-out and engage in child labour. We have to provide them non-formal education both in urban and rural areas. All these require the knowledge and skill of extension education.

Extension uses democratic methods in educating the people. It respects the individuality of people in making their own decision to the help of the extension worker. By this way, the people grow in status and self-respect and are able to take decisions rationally. Extension helps in the adoption of innovations. These innovations are of no use, unless they are put into practical use. It is through extension that these new findings can reach the people speedily. Rural problems are numerous and concerned with a large number of people spread over a large area. They can only be dealt with by an efficient extension agency meant for that purpose. The trained extension worker will understand the technology, to be transferred among the rural people by studying their problems.

### *Origin of Extension Education*

The word 'Extension' is derived from the Latin word, *tensio* meaning 'Stretching' and 'ex' meaning 'out'. Thus, the term 'extension education' means that type of education which is 'stretched out' into the villages and fields beyond the limits of the schools and colleges to which the formal type education is normally confined.

Extension education as a national policy and programme originated in the United States of America, in the days of Abraham

Lincon in response to the need for informal and practical out of school education for rural people.

The government granted land for the establishment of colleges for teaching agriculture and mechanical arts on condition that they should cater the needs of the surrounding population. Hence these schools were popularly called as "land-grant" colleges. These colleges specialise students in agriculture, and home economics.

The knowledge gained in the classroom and the laboratory of the extension service centre is extended to the farmers and the members of the families in every part of the country.

In India extension work had its beginning with a few outstanding individuals with a philosophic and philanthropic bent of mind. The work of most of them was necessarily confined to relatively small areas.

One of the pioneers of rural welfare work in India was the famous poet, Rabindranath Tagore. Tagore believed in both self-help and mutual help and was the first one to recognise the need for a change in the outlook of villages, as a pre-condition for improvement. Therefore, he urged that every villager and his family should be educated.

Tagor's Srinikethan Institute teaches subjects like agriculture, village welfare, co-operation, scouting, village industries and education attesting his insight into the needs of the villagers.

## A Review of History of Extension Programme

### *Pre-British Period*

During this period, the villages were self-contained, self-sufficient and self-governed units and there was little need for social welfare. This was disturbed by the invasions of foreigners and Mughal rule. When people felt the need for rural reconstruction work, the panchayat system provided some of these facilities but the development of centralised seats of the government made these unimportant.

### *British Period*

The series of famines from 1875 to 1901 forced the government to appoint some commissions. It recommended rural development work. It followed certain acts for the establishment of development departments like agriculture, animal husbandry and veterinary, irrigation, etc. In 1935, the rural development work was transferred as a provincial subject and as a result of this, several provinces established their rural construction departments or village uplifting boards.

### *Extension Activities by Other Agencies*

#### *Shantiniketan*

In 1908, Sri Rabindranath Tagore started youth organisation in the villages, in the Kaligram Pargana of his *zamindari*.

In 1921, he established a rural reconstruction institute at Shantiniketan. a group of 8 villages was the centre of the programme.

#### *Objectives of the Programme*

1. To create a real interest in people for rural welfare work.
2. To study rural problems and to translate conclusions into action.
3. To help villages, develop their resources, and
4. To improve village sanitation.

#### *Functions*

1. Developing village leadership.
2. Organizing village scout called Bharathi–Balika.
3. Establishing training centres for handicrafts, and
4. Establishing demonstration centres at Shantiniketan.

The Institute could not get much help from the government and it could not conduct research work. So, its work remained limited to the eight villages only. It has now been recognised as an important centre for research in extension work.

#### *Gurgaon Experiment*

Gurgaon experiment was organised by F.L. Bryne, Collector of Gurgaon district in 1920. He was prompted by the poverty and the misery of the people. The project emphasis was laid on increasing farm yields, curtailing expenditure on social and religious functions, improving health standards and organising welfare programmes.

'Village guides' were appointed in villages and they made extensive use of films, folk-songs, dramas, etc. to approach the people. He also encouraged the education of women.

Village guides were not technical men, but they merely served as channels for information from outside.

The experiment remained dependent upon the initiative of a single person, and when he is removed through transfer to another district, the people reverted to their traditional way of life. In 1933, Mr Bryne was appointed Commissioner for Rural Reconstruction in Punjab and his work was further expanded. The Punjab Government aided the work financially in 1935-36. Later, it was transferred to the Co-operative Department and 'Better living societies' were organised.

### *Shri Daniel Hamilton's Scheme of Rural Reconstruction*

In 1903, Sir Daniel Hamilton had experimented with mode village along cooperative lines in Bengal. This work was continued with the organization of a central cooperative bank and a cooperative marketing society. This later offered training in cottage industries through its rural reconstruction institutes.

### *Christian Missions*

The activities of the Christian Missionaries can be accounted under three major heads:

(a) Education

(b) Medical services

(c) Rural reconstructions.

### *Education*

Educational institutions run by these missions were about, 2000 elementary schools, 225 high schools and 38 colleges. In some of the colleges, there was a separate block attached to it for the extension work.

### *Medical Services*

There were mission hospitals, spread throughout the country which became effective centres for imparting training in medicine, nursing, compounding and mid-wifery and many students after receiving training in these institutions have established themselves in villages, to carry on their work.

### *Rural Reconstructions*

Several agricultural demonstration centres, at Marthandam, Ramnad, Patanchery and other YMCA and YWCA institutions have been doing useful work in rural areas.

### *Marthandam Attempt*

Marthandam project was started by Hatch at Travancore state in 1921 under the auspices of the YMCA. He was an American agriculture expert. The objective of the project was to bring about a complete upward development towards a more abundant life for rural people in spiritual, mental, physical, social and economic fields. The working principles of the project were self-help with expert guidance, training person to improve their performance, making people conscious of their wants and needs, and organizing reconstruction programmes to include the poorest. From the demonstration centre at Marthandam about 100 villages were covered through YMCA centres in villages. Most successful projects like egg-selling club, honey club, bull club, weavers' club, etc. had extensive social activities which could meet the needs of the villagers. It arranged exhibitions, lectures, and had a wide range of health programmes.

### *Gandhian Constructive Programme*

Regarding development work in the country Gandhiji empnasised that the salvation of India lies in villages. A key word of his economy are as follows:

1. Decentralised production and equal distribution of wealth.
2. Self-sufficiency of Indian villages.

He wanted to eradicate the class of middleman exploiters so that the farmers could get the full prices of their produce and he also wanted that the tillers should be able to consume their own products like fruits, milk, vegetables, etc. He formulated an 18-point programme which included the promotion of village industries, adult education, rural sanitation, uplift of backward tribes, women, education in public health, hygiene, economic equality, organisation of *kisans*, labour and student.

Gandhiji created leaders like Vinoba, Nehru, Jayaprakash Narayan, Meraben, etc. The Satyagrah Ashram at Sabarmati and

Sevagram in Wardha became not only places of training but of a pilgrimage.

### *Etawah Pilot Project*

Etawah Pilot Project programme was conceived and born in 1947 at Etawah in U.P. First 64 villages which later risen to 97 were covered under it. Albert Mayer of USA who came to India with American forces in 1944, was the originator of the project.

The main objectives of the project were to see what degree of production and social improvement initiative and co-operation could be obtained from an average area.

The pilot programe included introduction of improved agricultural and animal husbandary practices, public health education, literacy campaigns, improvement of cottage industries, training in repairing, and evaluating agricultural implements and all round village uplift activity.

### *Firka Development Scheme*

Firka development scheme was government sponsored scheme established in Madras States. It aimed at the attainment of the Gandhian ideal of Gram Swaraj. The scheme was launched in 1946, in 34 firkas throughout the states. In 1950, it was extended to another 50 additional firkas.

In order to effectively stimulate healthy competition between the official and non-official agencies, Government of Tamil Nadu decided to entrust the development schemes, to non-official agencies engaged in constructive work. Five non-official agencies were selected and paid grants, for doing firka development. These are as follows:

1. Rural reconstruction
2. Drinking water facilities
3. Sanitation
4. Agriculture, and
5. Khadi and village industries.

### *Nilokheri Experiment*

Nilokheri experiment was originally started to rehabilitate 7000 displaced persons from Pakistan and later integrated with the 100 surrounding villages into what came to be a rural-cum-urban township. In 1948, it was built round the vocational training centre that was transferred from Kurukshetra.

Sri S.K. Day was the central figure of this project, later Union Minister of Community Development and Co-operatives upto 1965.

The scheme called *Mazdoor manzil* aimed at self-sufficiency for the rural-cum-urban township in all the essential requirements of life—the colony has school, farm, polytechnique training centre, dairy, poultry farm, piggery farm, horticulture, garden, printing press, garment factory, engineering workshop, soap factory, etc.

### *Adarsh Seva Sangh (Pohri, Gwalior)*

This plan of rural reconstruction (Adarsh Seva Sangh) was put into action initially in 232 villages, falling in the Jagirdari of Col. Shitole which aimed to increase the per capita income of villagers. In each village, a Village Reconstruction Society was formed and the important items of work were compost making, deep ploughing, improved breeding and management of cattle, etc. The Sangh published a monthly journal *Rural India* which is devoted to planning and community projects.

### *Indian Village Service (IVS)*

The founder of IVS, Mr Arther T. Mosher of New York and Shri B.N. Gupta established it in 1954. The objectives of this organization were to assist village people to realize the best in their own villages, by developing individuals, volunteer leaders and local agencies and enable them to be effective in helping themselves and others. The objective also includes assisting government in developing villages.

For realization of the above objectives, the organization adopted techniques like personal contacts, informal discussion groups, use of volunteers, demonstrations, use and production of periodicals, etc. It is financially supported by contributions and donations. The organization has branches in Lucknow and Etah (UP) and is affiliated to the Presbyterian Church in the USA. Residents of 15 villages are the beneficiaries of this organization.

### *Sarvodaya Programme*

Sarvodaya programme was based on Gandhian conception and evoked great enthusiasm in Bombay state. The main features of this programme were simplicity, non-violence, sanctity of labour and reconstruction of human values. It aimed at raising the standard of living, a scientific development of agriculture, promotion of cottage industries, spread of literacy, medical and health facilities and the development of village panchayat.

# 3

# ALLIED CONCEPTS

Extension education is, 'education for people outside the regularly organized schools and classrooms for bringing out social and cultural development'. It aims at changing the outlook of people by educating them.

The term 'extension education' comprises of adult and informal education. It is concerned with educating the adult farmers or home makers or teachers in the techniques of raising better crops, raising better animals, better fruits trees managing home in a better way, rearing children scientifically, in taking care of the nutrition of the family and better communication and techniques of teaching. The various disciplines related to extension education programmes are as follows:

**(a) Agricultural Extension.** Extending knowledge to the agriculturists on agricultural practices.

**(b) Veterinary and Animal Husbandry Extension.** Extending knowledge about breeding, managing, feeding and care of animals and birds, etc.

**(c) Agricultural Engineering Extension.** Extending knowledge about the agricultural machinery like tractors, pumps, levelling of land, water use, soil conservation, etc.

**(d) Home Science Extension.** Extending the technical knowledge to ladies on food, child care, home decoration, kitchen gardening, etc.

**(e) Industry Extension.** Extending the knowledge on managing and running industries, and creating a good working relationship with the employees and employers so that the production could improve.

**Education Extension.** During early days, education centres were considered as ivory towers concentrating only on teaching and research. The days have now gone and the third dimension of extension is given priority. The fruits of education should perculate into the society and make everyone enjoy.

Through formal and non-formal systems we try to reach every one. Hence the slogan "education for all". To achieve this goal means not making everybody a graduate or a postgraduate, but make everyone a literatre or educated. This could be done through extension programme undertaken by education institutions.

Teacher education institutions can improve the quality of education at levels by providing in-service training to the teachers on the content and techniques of teaching.

Thus the ultimate aims of extension education in any field would be to bring about:

(a) Changes in knowledge or things known.

(b) Changes in skills or things done.

(c) Changes in attitudes or things felt.

## Extension Educational Process

Extension education is a service which deals with various strategies of change in the behavioural patterns of human beings through technological and scientific innovation for the improvement of their standard of living. The process of extension education has five essential phases. These phases show sequence of steps in a cycle that may be expected to result in progress from a given situation to a new or more desirable situation.

### *Phase I: Analysis of Situation*

Analysis of situation requires a large amount of facts about all aspects of the situation. Facts are needed about the people, their interests, education, what they think, they need, their social customs, habits and folkways. Facts are needed about the physical situation, such as soil, type of farming, markets, size of farms, cropping systems, housing condition, community services and communications. Some of these facts shape into problems—local, national and international. Other facts show the resources that are available through organizations and agencies. New facts and research findings should be introduced by the extension worker to stimulate a fresh approach to the problems of people. A thorough analysis will examine changing conditions and take a careful look ahead, comparing "what is" with "what should be".

***Phase II: Deciding Objectives***

It is necessary to distinguish between levels of objectives by separating the general objectives from the specific or working objectives. The planning process must enable the people to select a limited number of problems and to state their objectives.

***Phase III: Teaching***

Teaching involves choosing the following:

(a) The content or what is to be taught.

(b) Methods and techniques of communication.

Different methods of communication are used to create effective learning situations. These will be chosen from mass media, group, and personal methods. The ability to choose and use those methods best adapted to particular objectives is the measure of an extension worker's effectiveness.

***Phase IV: Evaluation***

Evaluation phase determines to what extent the objectives have been reached. This will also test how accurately and clearly the objectives have been stated. Plans for evaluation should be built into the plans of work during earlier phases. Distinction is made between more records of accomplishments and the process of comparing these results with the original objectives. The process of evaluation may be simple and informal or it may be formal and very complex.

***Phase V: Reconsideration***

Reconsideration phase consists of a review of previous efforts and results which reveal a new situation. If this new situation shows the need for further work, then the whole process may begin again, with new or modified objectives. Hence this process is continuous. The new situation is different because the people have changed. The physical economic, and social changes may have occurred, and the extension worker is better prepared to recognise new needs and interests.

## Scope of Extension Education

As stated by V.T. Krishnamachari,

"Extension is a continuous process designed to make the rural people aware of their problems and of indicating to them the ways and means, by which they can solve them. It involves not only education of the rural people in determining their problems and methods of solving them, but also inspiring them towards positive action in doing". Extension education is a science which deals with the creation, transmission and application of knowledge designed to bring about planned changes in the behaviour complex of people, with a view to help them live better by learning the ways of improving their vocations enterprises, and institutions.

As stated by Kelsey and Hearne, "Extension ...................... ........................ by doing".

The scope of extension education includes all the activities directed towards the development of people. The extension service must have dynamic programmes keeping pace with the constantly changing conditions in the society, scope of extension work in all the fields are indicated below, which suggest that extension education is a continuous process and not one-time job:

1. Increasing efficiency in agricultural production.
2. Increasing efficiency in the marketing, distribution and utilization of agricultural inputs and outputs.
3. Conservation, development and use of natural resources.
4. Proper management on the farm and in the home.
5. Better family living, science for the masses, environmental education, population education, providing legal literacy.
6. Youth development.
7. Leadership development and peace education.
8. Community and rural development.
9. Improving public affairs for alround development.
10. Making everyone literate, and
11. Improve the quality of educations and life.

### *Aims and Objectives of Extension Education*

The general aim of extension education is to provide a body of organized facts and generalizations that will enable teachers, researchers, extension workers and administrators to increasingly realise both cultural and professional objectives.

An analysis of general aims reveals many specific aims. Some of the most important aims are as follows:

1. To develop a conviction and general realization of the fact that growth can be promoted, learning acquired, social behaviour improved and personality adjustments effected. The realisation of this objective will produce an increasing appreciation of what extension education contributes to the teachers or extension educators.
2. To assist in defining and setting up extension educational objectives and standards in terms of desirable behaviour changes.
3. To aid in developing an impartial but sympathetic attitude towards, clientele, so that their behaviour will be observed objectively.
4. To assist in achieving a better understanding of the nature and importance of human relationships and the methods of developing these in clientele as well as such modes of functioning as getting along with others, participation in group efforts and co-operation.
5. To provide a body of facts and principles that can be used as problem-oriented and project-directed solutions.
6. To aid in affording the extension educators a better perspective for finding both the results of their own efforts and the practices of others.
7. To furnish the teachers with the necessary facts and techniques for analysing behaviour, both their own and that of others, so that normal adjustment may be facilitated and growth effected.
8. To assist in defining, maintaining and combining progressive extension methods, procedures and techniques for the sophisticated technologies in a simple and understandable form, to every one involved in extension education.

### *Specific Objectives*

1. To change the look-out of the villagers. Unless the people develop rising expectations for a higher level of living, there can be no motivation. Hence the people should have required leadership and assure that village development will become a continous people's programme.
2. To develop responsible and responsive village leadership of village organizations and institutions.
3. To help village people to become self-reliant, responsible citizens, capable and willing to participate effectively and with knowledge and understanding in the building of the nation.
4. To emphasis improving and modernizing agricultural practices and methods essential for increased agricultural production.
5. To improve existing and the new cottage industries and other small-scale industries for increasing the employment and to increase the earning.
6. To motivate the family members to satisfy their needs of food, clothing, shelter, recreation, health and religion.
7. To upgrade the competence and social status of the village teachers and to enable them participate in the community development programme.
8. To cut down the high death toll caused by illness, malnutrition, inadequate medical aids.

### *Philosophy of Extension Education*

The word 'philosophy' has a wide range of meanings. It was originally used to denote the love of wisdom or knowledge, theory or investigation of the principles or laws that regulate the universe and underlie all knowledge and reality.

1. According to Ensminger (1962) the philosophy of extension is changing the attitudes, knowledge and skills of the people and it is an educational process.
2. Extension is working with men and women, young people, boys and girls to meet their needs and wants. Extension is teaching people what to want and ways to satisfy their wants.

3. Extension is "helping people to help themselves".
4. Extension is "learning by doing" and "seeing is believing".
5. Extension is development of individuals, their leaders, their society, and their world as a whole.
6. Extension is working together to expand the welfare and happiness of people.
7. Extension is working in harmony with the culture of the people.
8. Extension is a living relationship, respect and trust for each other.
9. Extension is a two-way channel and it is a continuous, educational process.

Rudromurthy (1966) has linked the philosophy of extension work with the vedas, the upanishads, the Gita as well as the orthodox and unorthodox schools of philosophy. This is based on the concept of man and the values which are worthy of human pursuit.

Incidently, it was this philosophy of extension that was stressed by the late Prime Minister Nehru in the following words during his address to the National Development Council on November 8, 1963 in connection with the mid-term appraisal of the third plan.

"In the ultimate analysis, it is the human being that counts the human being, whether he is a minister or administrator, whether he is a man in the field or factory. All the machines in the whole world do not take the place of the human being. The human being makes the machine. The machine does not mould man ultimately. It is the human being that destroyed Germany, Japan and Russia and after the war, built it up again. In ten years period they became great powers and their production is increasing at top rate. Why is it so? Because of the human beings there. The average man is a trained man in those countries. They are all hard workers".

## Principles of Extension Education

The principles of extension are relative and not necessarily fixed in importance or sequence. Generally, however, it is also true that all the principles are important. It may also be relevant to point out that it is never possible to prepare a complete and final list of the extension principles. The principles discussed below are those which are either fundamental in nature or widely accepted in literature on the subject.

### *Principles of Interest and Needs*

To be effective, extension work must begin with the interests and needs, of the people. Many times the interests of the rural people are not the interests of the extension worker. Even though they see the needs of the people better than they do themselves, they must begin with the interests and needs as they (the people) see them.

### *Principle of Organization*

For extension work to be effective and real, it has to be a synthesis of democracy obtained at the level of family more particularly at the village level. Things must spring from below and spread like grass.

At the same time, modern science calls for an advanced stage of organization and a wiser co-ordination of thinking and action that is feasible in a single family or a single village. A higher level of living means wider specialization in a village. This calls for the corresponding organization of different professions and advocations. They have to be woven together at the level of the enlarged family at the village community level. The panchayats as social institutions, have also to be established at the block and the district levels. Thus, the establishment of the three-tier system, namely village panchayat, block-samiti and zilla parishad, followed by state legislatures and parliament satisfy the grassroots principle of organization in the extension.

### *Principle of Cultural Differences*

In order to make extension programmes effective, the approach and procedure must be suited to the culture of the people—different cultures require different approaches. A blue print of work designed to one part of the globe cannot be applied effectively to another part, mainly because of cultural differences. These differences can be perceived in the way of life of the people, their attitudes, values, loyalties, habits and customs.

### *Principle of Cultural Change*

The changed ways must be learnt and all learning must be grafted on what is already known, hence it is essential that the change agent who works personally with the villagers must know what the villagers know and what they think. With this in mind and with an attitude of mutual respect and respectiveness, the worker must seek to discover and understand the limitations, the taboos and the cultural values related to each phase of his programme, before it is introduced in order that an acceptable approach may be selected.

### *Principle of Cooperation and Participation*

Most members of the village community will co-operate in carrying out a project and if they helped to decide to undertake. It has been the experience of many countries that people become dynamic if they are permitted to take decisions concerning their own affairs, exercise responsibility for, and are helped to carry out projects in their own villages.

### *Principle of Laboratory to Land*

Applied agricultural science is not a one-way process. The problems of the people are taken to the scientists who do the experimentation necessary to find out the solutions. The extension workers translate the scientific findings of the laboratories in such a way that the farm families can voluntarily adopt them to satisfy their own needs. Taking the problems from field to the laboratory and from the laboratory to the field would be a suitable principle for better adoption by both.

### *Principle of Democratic Approach*

Extension work is democratic both in philosophy and procedure. It aims to operate through discussion and suggestion. Facts about a situation are shared with the people. All possible alternative solutions are placed before the participants, and their merits are highlighted through mutual discussions.

### *Principle of Learning by Doing*

In extension work, farmers should be encouraged to learn new things by doing and by direct participation. As Dr. Newman (1889) said "Farmers, like other people, hesitate to believe and set on theories, or even facts, until they see with their own eyes the proof of them in material form. We must in some way, bring this work to their personal attention. We must carry it home to them".

The motive for improvement must come from the people, and they must practice the new ideas by actually doing them. It is learning by doing, which is most effective in changing people's behaviour and developing the confidence to use new methods in future.

### *Principle of Trained Specialists*

It is very difficult for a multipurpose extension worker to keep himself abreast with all the latest findings of research in all the branches of science he has to deal with in his day-to-day activity. Trained specialists who keep themselves in touch with their respective research institutes on the one hand, and on the other hand, extend to the extension worker, the later scientific developments, which have scope for adoption in particular areas.

### *Principle of Adoptability*

No single extension teaching method is effective under all situations. Reading material is for those who come to the farms or homes where the demonstrations of recommended practices are conducted. Farms and home visits are by far, the most valuable, but they take up considerable time. New situations also arise where a special combination of method is necessary.

Similarly teaching the adult learners dropouts, needs a different techniques. Hence the use of teaching methods must have flexibility to be adopted to the members of a community who differ in age, education, economic status, sex, and proneness to change, etc.

### *Principle of Leadership*

A good rule in extension work is "never do anything yourself that you can get someone to do for you". This calls for the development of local voluntary leadership, and a participatory approach in extension programme.

The involvement of leaders in extension programmes is the one single factor that determines the success or failure of those programmes. Local leaders are the guardians of local thought and action and can be trained and developed to best serve as interpretors of new ideas to the villagers. If leaders are converted to new functions, the multiplication of new things to be done will almost certainly lead or drive them to share the role of leadership with others.

### *Whole Family Principle*

The family is the unit of any society. All the members of the family have to be developed equally by involving all of them. This is because of the following reasons:

(a) The extension programme affects the entire family.

(b) The family members have great influence in decision-making.

(c) It creates mutual understanding.

(d) It aids in money management.

(e) It balances farm and family needs.

(f) It educates the younger members.

(g) It provides an activity outlet for all.

(h) It unifies related aspects, such as the social, economic and cultural of the family, and

(i) It assures family service to the community and society.

It is not difficult to adopt this type of approach in extension programmes.

### *Principles of Satisfaction*

Satisfaction of the people or the beneficiary is very essential in extension work. Unless the people are satisfied with the end product of any programme, it is not going to be able to run. In democratic societies, people cannot remain like machines. They must continue to act on their own conviction and that is possible only when they drive full satisfaction through adoption of innovations well-suited to their needs and resources.

### *Guiding Principles for Successful Extension Work*

The following Do's and Don'ts may be taken to be a more or less comprehensive outline of the guiding principles for successful extension work.

1. Be thorough and uptodate in your professional knowledge and skills.

2. Be familiar with local conditions and practices including social background of people before you approach them.
3. Introduce yourself during your initial contacts and indicate the purpose of your visit.
4. Try to remember every villager or home maker or learner as a person, by their names.
5. Greet everyone you know and do it everywhere.
6. Make sure that you love villagers and you are sincerely interested in their welfare.
7. Identify yourself with the villagers and learners as much as possible.
8. Be informal and polite but neither too close nor too reserved.
9. Don't begin by giving undue promises of benefits.
10. Develop the art of listening.
11. Use simple, natural and local language which is meaningful to the learners.
12. Don't criticise or condemn the villagers or learners.
13. Avoid arguments.
14. Give credit to villagers and learners for their ideas or suggestions.
15. Admit your ignorance in the subject.
16. Don't correct a colleague or child or a subordinate in the presence of others.
17. Talk in term of the villagers' interest.
18. Begin with simple and common needs which can be easily fulfilled, without aiming at too high.
19. Don't try to solve villagers' problems for them, help the people to help themselves.
20. Insist the villagers or their representatives take part in preparing, executing, and evaluating plans at the family, village and block levels.
21. Use local leaders and co-operate with all people and organizations devoted to village improvement programmes.

22. Be behind the scene.
23. Whatever you do, try to complete it, so that you could win the confidence of the people.
24. Don't use any kind of compulsion.
25. Avoid giving anything free except your services.
26. Guide the villagers in securing the needed supplies and services.
27. Keep out of actions and politics.
28. Try to extend the benefits of extension to all groups and individuals.
29. While the visit is still fresh in your mind, you record what is observed during your visit.

### *Education and its Relationship with Other Disciplines*

Extension education is needed not just as an extension, it is an intimate part of an entity, a force greater than itself. This force is of a very dynamic nature and that is why it has established a deep-rooted and happy relationship with the majority of the biological and social sciences.

### *Extension Education and Social Sciences*

The student having a career interest in extension education is interested in acquiring knowledge about the various other disciplines, especially social sciences and their interrelationship with extension education.

### *Extension Education and Sociology*

Both, extension education and sociology have the same approach to groups. The immediate purpose of sociology is to study the structure, function and organization of the groups, while that of extension education is to study human behaviour in groups and also individual life, and how desirable changes can be introduced into them. But it is clear that neither extension education nor sociology can achieve this goal unless and until they seek the help of each other.

### *Extension Education and Rural Sociology*

Both these studies are closely oriented to the study of rural life. They work for the same cause of rural development and real the advantage of each others association.

### *Extension Education and General Psychology*

Extension education and general psychology are related because human behaviour in society cannot be studied until a thorough study of individual behaviour is made.

### *Extension Education and Social Psychology*

Both try to understand individual behaviour in a social situation. The fields under these two studies overlap each other.

### *Extension Education and Abnormal Psychology*

The study of abnormal psychology helps in understanding the anti–social behaviour of the people.

### *Extension Education and Cultural Anthropology*

Cultural anthropology studies human development and behaviour. One cannot deny the fact that from the findings of many anthropological studies, our attention has been directed towards the problems which extension education has to face.

### *Extension Education and Economics*

Both together work closely with reference to economic conditions prevailing in a particular group, or a particular individual.

### *Extension Education and Political Science*

In spite of the fact that many of the problems of political science and extension education are common in the fields of individual and group behaviour and in institutions of administrations, it should be remembered that both the subjects are not identical but help in each others growth.

### *Extension Education and Home Science*

Home science deals with education through which desirable changes are brought about in the family living. Extension education which works with almost every institution and all individuals who come from these families or home has a very happy relationship with the home science discipline.

### *Extension Education and Basic Education*

For the effective functioning of the extension education is basic understanding of its correlations with other allied disciplines. Both basic and extension educations aim at making men realise the highest aim of their life. They attach greater importance to the personality of the subject than to the tools and subjects or concepts taught. Both provide education which provides not only knowledge but also the practical skills for utilizing the knowledge.

Co-operation of the society is an essential factor for both basic and extension education. Evaluation for the continuous assessment of work done is considered to be more important to provide the needed feedback. Both insist productive work. Through extension and basic education one gets the education for life to formulate which improves the socio-economic status. They help rules of health and hygiene, sense of citizenship, adequate consciousness of rights and duties and healthy recreation suited to the needs of the community.

### *Extension Education and Adult Education*

Extension and adult education programmes are linked closely with regard to literacy component. The correct and scientific information on areas of agriculture, religion, social customs, etc. obtained through extension education programmes, can be utilized for adult education. Through these the rural as well as urban folk can understand the right perspective above personal matters of health, hygiene and farm family well-being natural phenomena like use of science and technology for increased productivity, better environment, checking population explosion and other such social problems.

The tribal population is yet another group of people who are away from the cultural, educational and economic mainstream of the society. Illiteracy, bonded labour, cultural disintegration, economic deprivation are the critical and elusive problems of tribal people. The adult education programme can establish link with these tribal group only through the extension programmes.

### *Extension Education and Non-formal Education (NFE)*

Non-formal education was made possible only through extension programme. Individuals could be educated and settle themselves well in life through NFE.

### *NFE for Rural Women*

Rural-based training in agriculture and agro-based industries, like dairying, poultry, rural-trades, village industries, handicraft, family welfare and health care are part of extension education programmes. These mainly cater to the needs of women.

Family welfare education includes child care, nutrition education, prevention of communicable diseases, population education, sanitation and hygiene.

These programmes are considered to be the major strategy for emancipating the rural underprivileged from social evils, economic deprivations, ignorance and superstition.

### *Functional Literacy and Extension Education*

Widespread illiteracy was considered to be the real handicap in the economic and social development of people. Therefore, a programme was proposed to plan and organise mass literacy movement to help increase the productivity in farm. The plan suggested that the adult literacy will have to be functional in character.

The functional literacy programmes were organized by agencies, like state departments of health, education, agriculture and youth organizations. At the district, block and village levels, development agencies like the health, agriculture, co-operation, banking, local panchayats and voluntary agencies provide support for these programmes.

### *Extension Education for Rural Women*

It is a well-known fact that the bulk of rural women clientele are the very poorer sections of the society. They face a lot of problems like malnutrition, lack of employment, economic dependence, exploitation in the hands of the male population and even the female elders in the family and the ignorance of protective legislation for women.

Some women's organizations which are involved in the functional literacy programme for women are as follows:

1. All India Women's Conference.
2. Centre for Women's Development Studies.
3. Bharatiya Grameen Mahila Sangh.
4. Indian Federation of University.
5. Indian Association for Women's Studies.

6. Kasturba Gandhi Memorial Trust.
7. National Council of Women in India.
8. National Federation of Indian Women.
9. Young Women's Christian Association of India and many were non-governmental agencies.

# 4

# RECENT TRENDS

India lives in her villages. This is a well-known fact. The concept of development in India thus become synonymous with the development of rural India where more than 75 per cent of the population live. Upliftment of rural areas is, therefore, crucial to the total development of the country. The planners and the policy makers should therefore, concentrate on the development of the villages first. This was concentrated in the Five Year Plans.

The universities, colleges and schools could provide institutional help, infrastructural facilities, training and demonstrations to the rural masses and thus spread the message of the concept of development and the recent trends in extension education. An educator should know the various schemes available for the poor to improve their socio-economic status so that the teacher as an extension worker could help them avail all these opportunities.

Agriculture is where most of our people, derive their livelihood and this sector, therefore, has the highest priority. Hence when the new strategy for agricultural development was adopted in 1966-67, the development programmes were revised to meet the needs of the farmer. Arrangements for the production and supply of improved seeds, particularly of the high yielding varieties, have been strengthened. Efforts were made to bring scientific and technological development closer to the farmer. The recent trends in the formation, organization, and conduct of development programmes are discussed in the following paragraph.

### *Agricultural Development Programmes*

Food is the primary necessity of every individual which means that it is inevitable to improve the agriculture. Our peasants, the landless labourers, the tribals, those who live in deserts and in other far-flung areas should know the difficulties involved and as well as our achievements in agriculture. It is our responsibility to make our farmers use the advancement in science and technology through constant interaction with them. In our anxiety to produce more we should not allow our farmers to use the fertilizers and pesticides more than the required amount and this spoil the fertility of the soil. The agriculture scientists should reach out to the peasants and spread the message required for a better cultivation. Following are some of the programmes organized by various agencies to improve farming.

### *Intensive Agricultural District Programme (IADP)*

The IADP was started on a pilot basis in 1961 in seven selected districts. The programme aims at combining technical know-how, credit and production supplies for stepping up agricultural production. IADP has contributed to a significant improvement in the use of critical inputs like improved seeds, fertilizers and plant production.

### *High Yielding Varieties Programme (HYVP)*

The cultivation of high yielding varieties since 1966-67 has resulted in a substantial increase in foodgrains production. For optimising the yield of available high yielding varieties of rice, it has been found necessary to advance their sowing time. The farmers were educated to raise nurseries and the programme gave encouraging results.

### *Drought Prone Areas Programmes (DPAP)*

This scheme formerly known as Rural Works Programme was initiated in 1970-71. It is a centrally sponsored scheme shared between the Central and the States Governments on 50-50 basis. Seventy-four districts were identified as drought prone and they have been grouped under 54 units. The programme aimed at mitigating the severity of scarcity conditions by executing rural works to generate employment. Some of the important elements envisaged in this integrated approach are changes in agronomical practices, restructuring the cropping pattern, and pasture development through proper management of small and marginal farmers and agricultural labourers.

Further the following suggestions are also made to improve the drought prone areas; improvement of eco-system soil and increasing conservation, changing the cropping pattern to suit the environmental factors, generation of employment, plantation activities both on private and government islands, tapping ground water resources and introducing animal husbandry programme.

### *Whole Village Development Programme (WVDP)*

For both special and functional integration of all programmes connected with agricultural production and reduction of unemployment, a new programme called the Whole Village Development Programme was implemented during the Fifth Five Year Plan period. Basic components of the programme are considerations of the proceedings in the village, overall land development planning through irrigation, support and restructuring of the cropping pattern.

## Sectoral Development Programmes

### *Tribal Development Blocks (TDB)*

For the development of tribal areas, 483 Tribal Development Blocks were functioning from March 31, 1974. The stress of this programme was on Integrated Area Development Plans which will combine the activities of TDB and other such tribal projects launched by the Government.

### *Pilot Project for Tribal Development (PPTD)*

This programme was launched in 1972-73 to study in depth, the problems of tribal areas relating to communications, administration, social services and economic development, especially agriculture.

### *Hill Areas Development Programmes (HADP)*

For all-round development of agriculture and improvement in the living conditions of the farmers in the hilly areas some pioneering projects were taken up in the states like Himachal Pradesh, Tamil Nadu and Uttar Pradesh. These programmes were called HADP.

## Animal Husbandry

### *Cattle and Dairy Development (CDD)*

The programmes for the development of animal husbandry and dairying aim at augmenting the supply of nutritive foods like milk, eggs and meat and helping the small and marginal farmers to diversify their economic activities. Cross-breeding of indigenous cows with bulls of exotic dairy breeds selective breeding were encouraged for augmenting milk production. Locating superior germ plans of important national breeds and opening Frozen Sem Banks was yet another programme which aimed at dairy development.

### *Sheep Development (SD)*

The Central Sheep Breeding Farms set up at Hissar with Australian assistance for corriedale breed of sheep had a flock strength of over 3,500 corriedale sheep. Under a centrally-sponsored scheme, establishment of large sheep-breeding farms in some selected states of the country were started under the fourth plan and the farms were fully established during the fifth plan.

### *Poultry Development (PD)*

Intensification of the scientific poultry breeding programme of Government farms has enabled the production of strain crosses which have given performance comparable to the exotic hybirds available in the country. The poultry industry, during this period, has attained sufficiency in producing genetically superior chicks.

### *Piggery Development (PIG D)*

All the eight modern bacon factories and pork processing plants established during the third and fourth plan period have been increasingly utilising their capacity for production of pork and pork products. Some of these factories have diversified their products and are handling different types of meat in addition to pork and pork products. Efforts are made to import pigs from abroad and introduce economic production units in the existing breeding stock.

### *Fisheries Development (Fr D)*

Development of fisheries have been assigned a high priority under the Fifth Five Year Plan in view of its vast potential for raising the nutritional levels of the protein deficiency. Indian diet and as a much needed foreign exchange.

## Integrated Rural Development Programme (IRDP)

The deliberations of the Indian Science Congress at its session held at Waltair (Andhra Pradesh) in January 1976, centred around the theme "Science and Integrated Rural Development: An Agenda for Action". As the result of the Congress the IRDP was started in India with the objectives of enabling selected families in rural areas to cross the poverty line.

The strategy of IRDP is to assist poorest of the poor and cover the less poor among them later in that order. This is based on the last man first principle. The IRDP is a centrally sponsored scheme funded by the Centre and the State on 50-50 basis. The objective of the programme is to assist poor families in villages to cross the poverty line by taking to self-employment. This is to be achieved by providing income generating assets to the youth through a package of assistance comprising subsidy and institutional credit.

TRYSEM—The Training of Rural Youths for Self-Employment Scheme is an important component of IRDP. It has been designed to provide training facilities to the rural youths between the age-group 15-35 who are below the poverty line, the technical skills and technical know-how to take up the self-employment in the areas of agriculture, farm-based industries, services and business activities. The target group should include a minimum of 30 per cent SCs/STs and 30 per cent women.

DWCRA—Development of Women and Children in Rural Areas is another sub-scheme of IRDP started by Government of India in 1982, during the Sixth Five Year Plan. The main objective of the scheme is to help the women to make use of the facilities available under IRDP, either individually or in a co-operative basis as small groups. A grant of Rs.15,000 was given as a revolving fund which was shared by Central Government, State Governments and UNICEF.

### *District Rural Development Agency (DRDA)*

In 1980 the Integrated Rural Development Programme was extended to all the development blocks of the country. The target set for IRDP was to assist on an averge 600 families in a block from the identified target group, in a year and to at least 3,000 families during the Sixth Plan period. Following this, it was decided that there should be a single agency which will be responsible for the implementation of all programmes viz. IRDP, DPAP, DDP, TRYSEM, Special Livestock Production Programmes and Programme for Women and Children, etc. so as to minimize administrative expenditure and result in better utilization of inputs included the personnel. Since this agency was established district level, it was called District Rural Development Agency (DRDA).

## Council for Advancement of People's Action and Rural Technology (CAPART)

CAPART encourages, promotes and assists voluntary action in the implementation of projects for the development of rural areas.

As a result of large-scale infrastructural development for conducting research in both farm and non-farm sectors, the quantum of technology evolved by the institutions could not be transferred to the users, which became a serious problem. To hasten this process a new project, viz. National Agricultural Research Project was launched in the year 1974 by ICAR. In the non-farm sectors, institutions like IIT's, polytechnics, CSIR, etc. evolved technologies which could not even touch the fences of the institution and mostly remained in laboratories for want of proper mechanism of transferring the same to users. Hence, a new institution with the name, Council for Advancement of People's Action and Rural Technology (CAPART) has sanctioned number of projects to organization of beneficiaries for antipoverty programmes. They are sponsored by voluntary agencies. All the rural development programmes organized by voluntary agencies aimed at improving the living conditions of the poor and to promote their productivity too.

## National Agricultural Research and Extension Projects

To accelerate the pace of agricultural development as a whole and to consolidate the isolated efforts made through launching several programmes, projects and schemes so far and to bridge the gap between research and extension addressed to overcoming the specific localised and problem-oriented approaches, the Government of India launched two specific projects with the financial and technical assistance from the International Development Bank, viz. (i) National Agricultural Research Project and (ii) National Agricultural Extension Project.

*National Agricultural Research Project (NARP)*

The NARP is the first major effort of ICAR to upgrade and strengthen the regional research capability of the State Agricultural Universities. The project is designed to fill the gaps in research and also to meet the needs of extension services and farmers as far as new and proven technologies generated through applied research addressed to specific localised constraints in agricultural production are concerned.

*National Rural Employment Programme (NREP)*

The problem of poverty is directly related to the existence of unemployment, under-employment and low productive employment.

Based on the remarkable success of NREP project and as a result of realizing the further widening gaps in the extension services, the NREP project was launched. NREP projects tries to overcome the various organizational and functional constraints identified earlier and tries to rectify many of them.

## Environment Education Programme

To preserve and protect the environment a lot of efforts have been taken up by the NGOs and the Government. The Ministry of Environment and Forests serves as the modal agency in the administrative structure of the Central Government for the planning, promotion and co-ordination of the environmental and forestry programmes. The following are the main activities of the Ministry. Conservation and survey of flora, fauna, forest and wildlife; prevention and control of pollution, afforestation and regeneration of degraded areas and protection of environment. These tasks are being fulfilled through environmental impart assessments, eco regeneration, assistance to organizations implementing environmental and forestry programmes; promotion of environmental and forestry research, extension education and training to augment the requisite manpower, dissemination of environmental information, international cooperation and creation of environmental awareness among all sectors of the country's population.

The NGOs have their own activities to create awareness among the people the need for protecting the environment from pollutions. They organize campaigns, and environment education through eco clubs and other activities in the communities.

Indian Institute of Forest Management (IIFM), Bhopal is an autonomous body of the Ministry which imparts education and training in forest management aims at inculcating professionalism in forestry management.

It offers regular and short-term courses in forestry management, farm forestry management, integrated watershed management, sustainable management of forest resources, etc.

Indira Gandhi National Forest Academy (IGNFA) Dehradun is a premier forestry training institution of the country imparting in service training to IFS probationers. The Wildlife Institute of India (WII) provides in-service training in wildlife management to forest officers, wildlife ecologists and various other professionals.

### *Formal Environmental Education*

The Ministry is continuing its interaction with University Grants Commission (UGC), National Council of Education Research and Training (NCERT), Department of Education, Ministry of Human Resource Development (MHRD), etc. for implementing programmes relating to environmental education.

### *Non-formal Environmental Education and Awareness*

The Ministry provides priority for the promotion of non-formal environmental education and creation of awareness among all sections of the society through diverse activities using traditional and modern media of communication.

## Centres of Excellence

The Ministry has set up five centres of excellence with a view to strengthening awareness, research and training and training in priority area of environmental science and management.

Centre for Environmental Education (CEE), Ahmedabad set up in 1984 continue to develop and carry out nationwide environmental education.

CPR Environmental Education Centre (CPREC), Chennai was set up in 1988 with the objective of creating and increasing consciousness and knowledge about the environment and to generate resource national and educational packages on environmental conservation.

Centre for Ecological Sciences, Bangalore was established in 1983 with the aim of focussing on the ecology and environment of the Western Ghats.

Centre for Mining, Environment, Dhanbad was established at the Indian School of Mines with the objectives of training the field personnel to environmental science and technology with reference to environmental management in mining areas.

Salim Ali Centre for Ornithology and National History (SACON) was established in 1990 with the major objective of conducting research and post-graduate level courses on all aspects of ornithology (scientific study of birds) and national history of other life forms.

# 5

# QUALITIES OF WORKER

The efficiency and performance of any organization depends directly on how effective its manpower is and how well they are trained for the purpose. Training is concerned with not only imparting specific skills for particular purposes and also creating interest and an aptitude for the job.

When we say 'extension worker' it refers to all persons working in the extension field, like village level workers, the extension officers and block development officers, extension specialist, home scientist and the teachers of formal and non-formal education. An extension worker is bound to touch upon all aspects of life and has a multipurpose role to play.

## Qualities of an Effective Extension Worker

To play the role successfully, the extension worker, has to have the following qualities:

An extension worker must be resourceful and must have thorough knowledge of the subjects with which he is concerned and must be able to respond well to the questions asked; must be honest, sincere and hard-working; should have self-confidence and be able to judge things and incidences correctly; should be sympathetic and a partner in the joys and sorrows of people; should have the determination to achieve the goal set and should make all attempts in that direction; should be innovative and move towards the positive end; should have an urge to complete the task undertaken; should be in a position to visualise the future plans and programmes; resourceful enough to approach various agencies for help; should be able to face the difficult situations and take decisions on his own; should be humble, polite and friendly to the people; should listen to others, respect their feelings: think over the problems and suggest appropriate solutions; should have the attitude to serve others; should be able to guide the people; should be able to prepare and use as many teaching aids and techniques as possible to make people understand better; should first listen to others and then start talking slowly after knowing the minds of the people, should not be hastened in pressing his views first and should always be a seeker of new ideas, knowledge and techniques to spread the message to the people, should keep well-informed about the latest developments in the various disciplines in the community in which he is to work; establish rapport with the clientele; have a clear understanding of the role of the extension service and how it operates; should possess the ability to plan effectively and quickly; know the social belief of the people; remain motivated in odd situations; accept failure sportively; able to recognise the felt need of the people; able to evaluate the methods and achievements of programmes; able to move and adjust with people; and should be able to correspond with local leaders.

## Need for Training

It is felt that a young person entering a career will have to be trained for two or three professions in the span of their active lives of work. This is because many new developments will render much of today's knowledge obsolete.

The professional worker must keep abreast of the latest development in his field, otherwise he will soon be working far below his potential and capacities.

Training improves a person's skill, his/her power of intelligence and develops in him the desired attitudes and values required for his/her work. Training helps the new entrant to acquire occupational work skills and the latest knowledge, makes him/her familiar with the objectives of the organization to which he belongs and helps to make his potential contribution in promoting the goals of his organization. Training also makes up for any deficiencies in the new recruits and maintains or boosts up the morale of the staff. It is conducive to adhesion in regard to methods of work and approach to problems.

Training has special significance in the field of agricultural development and in the context of community development extension since the very essence of these programmes is to train rural people to solve most of their problems individually or in groups. The success of the extension worker can be judged ultimately by the extent to which he has been able to make the village people self-reliant in getting them to do things by themselves, without relying on outside help.

Ensminger has stated that it is not enough to agree that all staff-administrators, specialists, village extension workers should be trained in the methods of extension education. To be trained in extension for community development means according to him, first to understand the philosophy and objectives of community development; second, to understand what is meant by extension; third, to know what can be expected from the correct use of extension; fourth, to know how to apply extension methods and finally, to know how to evaluate the effectiveness of the extension methods used.

It has been pointed out that extension involves not only educating the rural people in determining their problems and methods of solving them, but also inspiring them towards positive action.

## Training

Training means to educate a person so as to be fitted, qualified proficient in doing some job. For an extension worker, training includes education which aims at bringing a desirable change in the behaviour of the trainee, or the learners. Training has been defined by Milton Hall as, "the process of aiding employees to gain effectiveness in their present or future work through the development of appropriate habits of thought and action, skills, knowledge and attitudes".

Training is not the idea of knowledge received, but that of such knowledge digested through application, drill and discipline. It means getting a man to do a job correctly, effectively and consciously so that he can do or apply what he has learnt effectively, can produce the desired results.

## Education Versus Training

Lynton and Pareek discussed the relationship of training to other related areas such as education and learning. According to them, education is primarily concerned with opening out the world to the students so that they can choose their interests mode of living and also their career. Training, on the other hand, is primarily concerned with preparing the participants for certain lines of action which are delineated by technology. Education deals with knowledge and understanding whereas, training deals with understanding and development of skills.

In a restricted sense, 'training' may be taken to connote the acquisition of knowledge, skills and attitudes needed specifically for performing a particular job, whereas 'education' may refer to all sorts of acquisitions, with or without a pre-specified purpose or job, to be performed.

## Types of Training for Extension Workers

The training of extension worker can be classified as follows:

### *Pre–service Training*

The training is given to an extension worker receive before joining the actual job. This includes his education at a high school, or higher secondary school, a general college or professional college, viz. agricultural university, agricultural college, veterinary college, etc. where the extension worker receives degrees of B.Sc., B.Sc. (Ag.), B.V.Sc. etc., and the specific training as in case of a village level worker at the VLW Training Centre.

### *In-service Training*

This is for improving the ability by obtaining latest knowledge, or giving him some special training in the new job he is required to do. This may be orienting the new worker after he joins the job induction training, job training, short–range courses, periodical meetings and conferences, seminars workshop, etc.

*Orientation of New Entrants.* The worker when joins the job he needs to be oriented to the organizational set-up where he has to work, the philosophy behind the organization, the code of conduct, e.g. the extension and CD workers have to have training in the correct approach to the farmer, his relationship the ways of doing things, facilities he will get, reports he is to submit, broad principles of extension work, etc. For this purpose there are some orientation and study centres.

*Induction Training.* Some institutions have been designed where extension workers can be given knowledge of the working and organization of community development and extension service, his place of work and his place in the work-team. The orientation centres do this job.

*Short-Range Courses.* The Directorate of Extension in the Ministry of Food and Agriculture and Community Development through the State Agriculture and Veterinary Departments and Agricultural Colleges and Universities organizes 45 days training at Agricultural and Veterinary Colleges. They are given training in technical subjects like latest varieties and cultural practices, plant protection, use of fertilizers, etc.

*Job Training.* If the extension workers are required to do some special job like soil cover conservation or landscaping, they may be deputed to get this special training being given at some specially designed centres. In soil conservation it may be at Dehasadur forest in UP, or at Kota in Rajasthan, etc. NSS programme officers in schools and colleges are given periodical training to undertake the extension work to be undertaken by them with the assistance of the students.

*Periodical Meetings and Conferences.* Agricultural Universities, now organize such training in collaboration with State Agricultural and Veterinary Departments, for Extension Officers, working at District Level or above. *Rabi* and *Kharif* meetings are held to work out the package of practices for various districts for the coming crop seasons.

### *The Process of Training*

Lynton and Pareek divided the process of training into three phases, i.e. pre-training, training and post-training.

*Pre-training.* No previous experience is needed for the trainee as he is a fresher and hence he usually accepts whatever he is offered as his need. The participants motivation and point of view will determine his focus of attention and learning.

*Training.* In addition to the work-experience which the in-service training participant brings to the programme his expectation and explores in the training situation the subjects that interest him. The training institutions basic task is to provide the necessary opportunities to solve the job problems and meet his expectations. Having explored, the participant tries out some new behaviour. If the participant finds the new behaviour in the training situation. If he does not find it useful, he discards it and tries an alternative one.

*Post-Training.* When implementing what the extension worker has learned during his training session, he finds a changed situation and there begins a process of adjustment. The participant should be encouraging, and help him to use his training and offer him additional support of continuing contact with the training institutions.

### *Effective Extension Training*

Some basic principles for an effective extension training are given below:

*Motivation.* It is basic to good training. A good trainer must start his/her work by creating a feeling of need or want in the trainee since the actual willingness and desire to learn come from within the person. Basic needs, wants, desires, motives, incentives or urges have been classified broadly four ways.

(a) The desire for security—economic, social, psychological and spiritual.

(b) The desire for new experience—adventure, new interests, new ideas, new friends and new ways of doing things.

(c) The desire for affection and response—companionship gregariousness and social mindedness; the need for feeling of belonging.

(d) The desire for recognition—status, prestige, achievement and being looked upto.

*Defined Objectives.* Good training requires specific and clearly defined objectives. The different aspects of the training objectives, namely the persons to be trained, the behavioural changes to be developed in them, the content or subject-matter to which the behaviour is related and the real situation in which the changes are to take place must be clearly spelled out in the training objectives.

*Educational Changes.* Good training must accomplish certain kinds of educational changes in relation to the subject matter learned. These may be change in knowledge, or things known; changes in skills or ability to do new things, including mental skills and manual or physical skills; and issues, points of view, etc. including changes in interest and changes in understanding.

*Effective Learning Situation.* Good training requires effective learning situations which include for major elements, viz. teacher, learner, subject-matter, teaching-aids and facilities or environment.

*Effective Learning Experience.* Good training should provide effective learning experience to the trainees.

*Training Technique.* Good training requires usually a combination of training techniques. Training should involve appropriate activities engaging the maximum number of senses and a combination of techniques such as oral, visual, audio-visual and doing things.

*Challenging and Satisfying.* Training should be challenging and satisfying. To be challenging subject-matter must be presented in the form of problems for which the trainees should be encouraged to find solutions. Appropriate and timely recognition should be given to the trainees achievements. Fear and ridicule have no place in the training processes and their use in a training programme is usually an adverse reflection on the ability of the trainer.

*Evaluation of Results.* Good training requires careful evaluation of results.

### *Agencies of Training*

There are different agencies both governmental and non-governmental involved in training the extension workers for different activities. This covers the training of farmers and their sons, auxillary courses for poultry keepers, dairymen, kitchen gardeners and fruit preservation. Non-formal and adult education, literacy education, women and child welfare, etc.

### *Training of the Farmers*

Besides the national demonstrations, maximization demonstrations and other activities of the extension workers in the villages, there is a regular farmer training programme in all agricultural universities. The training includes crop-raising, animal-feeding management, plant protection.

### *Training for Farmer's sons*

In each state there are two or three Farmer's Sons Training Centres. In Madhya Pradesh there are four such training centres at Rewa (Kuthalia Farm), Gwalior, Raipur and Jabalpur. The procedure for such training is :

(i) The applicant who wants to receive training should himself be a farmer and should not be interested in service.

(ii) He is given free boarding and lodging and second class rail or bus fare both ways.

(iii) The duration of the course is five weeks. The young Farmers Association of India, New Delhi runs some of these centres. Punjab Agricultural University runs a school for farmer's sons.

### *Directorate of Extension (Department of Agriculture)*

The Directorate of Extension have taken up the following programmes for farm youth.

*Pilot Young Farmers clubs around Extension Training Centres:* With the start of the Community Development Programme in India the Directorate of Extension took up the responsibility of training the Gram Sevaks and Grama Sewakas in rural youth activities and women and child welfare programmes. So that after training they could organize these programmes in the Development Blocks. In order to provide them project oriented training in this aspect, ten pilot Young farmers' clubs were organized in selected villages in each of the development blocks attached to the extension training centres. The staff and trainees of the extension training centres organize training for the club members in leadership development, organizational aspects, skill development in the field of agriculture, and project activities. After training a regular follow-up is done to provide continuing education and guidance.

*Training of Young Farmers in Districts:* A massive programme of farmers training and education have been taken up in selected districts. There will be programme like demostration-cum-training camps, short duration training courses and discussion groups.

*Training Young Farmers through Voluntary Organizations:* National level farmers voluntary organizations are being encouraged to take up training programmes for the benefit of young farmers by organizing short duration training courses, seminars and exchange visits. Financial assistance is being provided to the six national level organizations by the Directorate of Extension, Government of India to enable them undertake programmes relating to agricultural production.

*International Farm Youth Exchange Programme with the USA and Countries other than the USA:* The Directorate of Extension in India has taken up this programme in collaboration with the National 4-H Club Foundation of the USA with a view to providing an opportunity to promising farm boys and girls to visit the USA to study modern methods of Agricultural Production, the rural Youth Programme and leadership development. This programme was then extended to other countries also.

*Exchange of Farmers within the Country:* This scheme is being implemented through the National Level Farmers Voluntary Organizations. Under this scheme young farmers from one area are being encouraged to visit other where considerable progress in the field of agriculture has been made.

*Regional Rural Youth Staff and Leaders Training Workshop:* In order to provide training in Rural Youth Development to the trainees of the Extension Training/Farmers Training Centres and Voluntary Youth Leaders, a National Workshop in collaboration with FAO was organized.

*People's Action for Development in India (PADI)–Department of Agriculture:* The PADI received aid from FAO and other donor countries to provide assistance to voluntary organizations and training institutions for taking up programme for rural youth development and young farmers training.

*Indian Council of Agricultural Research (ICAR) and Extension Worker Training:* Indian Council of Agriculture Research is an apex body involved in training the extension workers and personnels at various levels. It has 31 research institutions and helps 22 agricultural universities functioning in the country. Some of these institutions and universities have taken up research studies on the rural youth development programme while others have taken up rural youth field projects in selected villages. In addition ICAR has established Krishi Vigyan Kendras.

***Krishi Vigyan Kendra (Farm Science Centres)***

In pursuance of the recommendations of the Education Commission (1964-66) to establish institutions for providing vocational education in agriculture at the pre and post-matriculate level, the Indian Council of Agricultural Research has started a scheme to establish Krishi Vigyan Kendras (KVK) in the country. The main objectives of KVK are as follows:

(1) The Kendras will impart learning through work experience and hence will be concerned with technical literacy the acquisition of which does not necessarily require as a precondition the ability to read and write.

(2) The Kendras will impart training only to those extension workers who are already employed, or to practising farmers.

(3) There will be no uniform syllabus. Instead, the syllabus will be tailored according to the felt needs, natural resources and potential for agricultural growth.

***Rural Development Department***

The 'Yuvak Mandals' organized under the rural youth programme by the rural development department trains the youth club members to become better farmers, home makers and leaders.

***Department of Education (Youth Services Wing)***

The Department of Education in the State and Human Resource Development ministry have set up a youth services wing to look after the development of youth programme in the country. Some of them are as follows :

*Nehru Yuvak Kendras:* These Kendras were primarily designed to provide a forum for the non-student youth, particularly in rural areas, with a view to giving them the opportunities to participate in the development process.

*National Service Scheme (NSS):* The scheme provides for utilization of leisure time activities of students in various items of social work and national development activities, to create a sense of responsibility and social commitment.

### *Department of Social Welfare*

Department of social welfare has taken up rural youth programmes as far as it relates to pre-vocational training programme for school drop-outs. These centres have been established with a view to provide training in engineering trades.

### *Ministry of Labour*

Ministry of labour has taken up a scheme for providing craftmanship training to rural youth in various fields, including agro-industries, at their vocational training centres.

Training centres of these kinds should always serve as symbol of things good and progressive in community development. They should strive to set and demonstrate desirable standards in every respect and should in part be judged by the criterion. The quality of the centres depends upon the quality of the trainers and the institutional facilities available in relation to the objectives of the training programme.

# 6

# METHODS AND TECHNIQUES

The important task of extension is to extend the ideas what one has to others. The process of extending and exchanging ideas will be possible through effective communication. The extension teaching methods are the means through which the extension worker can communicate his ideas. The ideas may be conveyed either to an individual or a group of people.

Learning requires effective teaching. Effective teaching requires certain special aptitudes and skills on the part of teacher. These skills include the knowledge of technology or what to teach (an understanding of the educational process) or how to teach (skill with extension teaching methods) and the ability to work with village people. As Eator had rightly stated, "What the teacher desires, believes and thinks, teaches no one. He can accomplish his ends only by putting before his learners what they can understand, what they can do, in short, acts to bring learners into contact with stimuli selected and ordered according to his purpose".

Development in any field would never become self-sustaining unless it was accompanied by the corresponding changes in attitudes, values, knowledge and skills of the people. These can be accomplished only through education extended to all. National development and development of human potential depend on how well participate in the process of national development and contribute to it. This will become a reality through extension programme undertaken by all the agencies involved in development programmes.

The following are various extension teaching methods and here these are classified according to their use.

### *Individual Contacts*

Farm and home visits, office calls, personal letters, observation plots, results demonstration and telephonic conversation.

### *Group Contacts*

Demonstration meetings, leader training meetings, lecture meetings, conference and discussion meetings, meetings at result demonstrations, tours, schools, and miscellaneous meetings.

### *Mass Contacts*

Builetins, leaflets, newspapers, circular letters, radio, television, exhibition, and posters.

### *How to select teaching tools*

Though there are various extension training methods, one should always remember that the combination of several methods will be more effective than one particular method. We should not be concerned with choosing the best, but rather in choosing the right method for the right type of work. While working for the selection of a method, some considerations which should enter into our thinking are as follow:

The people to be educated, the target learner, the objective of the programme, the content of the programme, availability of resources for teaching, time duration, the sex of the audience, age, education, motives and other complex human characteristics and customs of the people to be reached; general local conditions, such as seasonal work, weather conditions, availability of meeting places, organization and leadership; financial and other resources available, and the competence of the instructors to use the techniques.

Though this is just a suggested list, it is very important to use the right method, in the right proportion at the right time, to the right person and by the right person.

## Individual Contacts

### *Farm and home visits*

It is a fact to face type of individual contact by the extension worker with the farmer and/or the members of his family on the latter's farm or at his home for one or more specific purpose connected with extension.

### *Objectives of Farm and Home Visits*

To obtain first-hand information on matters relating to farm and home conditions, to give advice or otherwise assist to solve a specific problem, or to teach skills, etc., to arouse the interest of those not reached by other methods, to select local leader demonstrators and other resource persons and to promote good public relations.

### *Procedures to be followed*

1. Decide upon the place of the farm and home visit in the teaching plan outlined, to advance a particular phase of the extension programme, decide whether the visits are primarily for direct teaching or to increase the effectiveness of group methods and mass media.
2. Clarify the purpose of the visit.
3. Planning for the visit—before you make a visit to either a farm or a home or to any place for extension you should keep in mind the following points and plan thoroughly:

Review the previous contacts made with members of family or the groups, check subject matter information likely to be needed and the reading materials like books, leaflets bulletins, etc. work out schedule of visits in consultation with the community. Remote and unfrequented farms and homes should always be kept in view, and consider best approach in view of the individual family situation.

4. What should you remember while making a visit?
   (a) Punctuality should always be borne in mind while visiting. Contact the people preferably when they are on the job. Be friendly, sympathetic and complimentary, gain and deserve interviewee's confidence,

allow the farmers to interact with you, peak only when the receiver is willing to listen, talk in terms of his interest, use natural and easy language, speak slowly directly and cheerfully, be accurate and correct in your statements, don't prolong arguments, complement the clients for good ideas and encourage them be sincere in learning as well as teaching, arouse interest and create a desire to take action, render the farmer a real service, leave clear impression in the minds of people, if possible, hand over some reading materials relating to the topic discussed. This will help in developing friendship; and leave the farmer or home maker as a friend.

5. Record the date, purpose of visit, what was accomplished and follow-up activities.
6. Follow-up activities—send applicable literature or other things by post or by other means, extend invitation to attend a meeting, if any, on the related topic, and make subsequent visits if and when required.

### *Advantages of visits*

Provides extension worker with first-hand knowledge of farm and home conditions and the viewpoints of farm people if made on request, the farmer or home-maker is likely to be ready to learn; the ratio of 'takes' (acceptance) to 'exposures' (efforts) is high, when we meet directly; builds confidence between the extension worker and the farmer; will be of support the effectiveness of group methods and mass media; contributes to selection of better local leaders, resource persons cooperators; promote good public relations; and is useful in contacting those who do not participate in extension activities and who are not reached by massmedia.

Home or farm visit also has certain limitations as listed below: Number of contacts is, limited; comparatively costly; and time of visit may not be always according to the convenience of the people.

### *Office Calls*

To facilitate quick solution to the problems of farmers, home makers and others; the extension worker can discuss and give necessary advice to them; to arrange for or ensure timely supply and services; to promote close contact between the beneficiaries and extension organization.

### *Principles to be Followed*

Office should be located convenienty so as to facilitate large number of people to visit easily, space and furniture should be arranged to permit orderly routing of visitors. There should be provision for caller to confer privately with the extension worker; officer room should be kept attractive with bulletin board; leaflets; office should be kept open during usual working hours; extension worker should regularly attend office while at headquarters. Arrangements should be made to provide information to the callers in the absence of the worker; cordial and sincere interest should be shown to visitor's problem; applicable reference materials, including record of previous contacts should be readily accessible; there should be unhurried consideration of the entire problem of the caller and the caller should be made to feel welcome to call again when there is necessity.

The extension worker should rather use that unfinished business connected with the call is completed as promised.

### *Advantages of Office Visits or Calls*

When the farmers or home maker and others make visits to the office the learing become most receptive as the demands for solving the problems come from them. As it saves time of the extension workers he/she could, concentrate on solving more problems and it also increases the good relation between the extension worker and the beneficiaries.

### *Limitations*

Extension worker cannot be at headquarters always. Callers in her/his absence may not be satisfied with the information or guidance obtained. Office contacts removed from actuality of farm or home situation may not reflect the real problem of accurately reveal the conditions of the problems; and visits are likely to be limited to those participating in other extension activities.

### *Personal Letters*

It is a personal and individual letter written by the extension worker to farmers or home maker in connection with the programme.

Under the existing conditions of high percentage of illiteracy, this extension method is relatively not very popular in India. A few people write to the extension worker for advice. Moreover, with obvious increase in the number of literates in rural India, and the involvement of educated youth in extension activities this method mav assume more importance in future.

### *Objectives*

To answer enquiries from the agriculturalists regarding specific farm problems, or supplies and services, etc. To seek the co-operation of farmers, home makers and others.

| | |
|---|---|
| (a) Courteous | – tone appropriate for the desired response. How something is said as important as what is said. |
| (b) | – give all necessary information to accomplish its purpose. |
| (c) Concise | – say what the extension worker has to say in the fewest words with clearness, completeness and courtesy. |
| (d) | – so that it is not only understood but cannot be misunderstood. |
| (e) | – contain to misstatement of facts, figures or grammatical errors, etc. |
| (f) Near | – free from overwritings, strikings, etc. |
| (g) Readable | – short sentences, short words, and human interest make for easy reading. |

### *Principles of Writing Letters to the Beneficiaries*

*Promptness.* A letter asking for information should be answered promptly because the person writing letter has more interest in passing on the matter and will be likely to use the information which provides a satisfactory solution to his problem. Remember that information delayed is information denied.

*Put yourself in the other fellow's shoes.* Have a genuine concern for the other fellow's interest, viewpoint, limitations and desires.

### *Advantages*

All letters can preserved and used for future reference purposes. Comparatively cheap; accurate information and minute details can be given, can be made easy and enjoyable to read, can be used to maintain or increase the tempo of work; can be used to continue the contacts; and can also promote literacy.

### *Limitations*

Limitations are of little use in areas of low literacy; cannot be used in exclusion of other methods, will lose its significance if not carefully prepared and used.

### *Observation Plots (District Trials/Minikit Trials)*

Suitability of a new practice in the field or at home is determined by this method.

A new practice means the introduction of a practice not existing hitherto, e.g., the teaching of prawn culturing, the introduction of an improvement over local practice, use of smokeless *chullah*, use of toilet; replacing already established improved practice with a more improved new practice. Introducing new techniques of teaching, use of electronic media in teaching, etc.

### *Objectives*

To test the performance under specified condition, of a new practice which has been found to be promising on a research situation or laboratory, to avoid possible losses economically and consequent loss of their confidence in extension due to large-scale introduction of new practises without prior observations to a small-scale; to build the confidence of both the extension worker and the user—the utility as well as feasibility of a new practice.

### *Principles*

Determine the need for arranging the observation plot, be clear about the specific purpose of the trial, select about six representative centres for conducting the trial, in these centres, select the co-operators in consultation with the local people or officers. Selection should be representative, co-operative and easily accessible, make it clear to the co-operator and to the other learners that it is a trial and an experiment only and not a demonstration plot, it is important that all operations are done under the personal supervision of the extension worker, restrict the size of the 'control' and experiment only and not a demonstration plot. Experiment groups to the minimum possible, so as to have large number of replications. Visit the place as frequently as possible and record on the spot and, recording should be accurate.

### *Advantages*

Avoid the pitfalls of hasty recommendation and/or adoption of new practices, constitutes the first step towards the spread of a new practice after thorough testing. Analysing the technicalities, difficulties and delays involved in laying out regular trial plots and analysing the results statistically, build confidence of the extension and research workers on the one hand and of the learners on the other, in the utility and feasibility of a new practice.

### *Limitations*

It makes heavy demand on the time and energy of extension worker, difficult to secure suitable co-operators sometimes risk of failure of a new practice resulting in financial loss to the co-operating client, conclusions may not always be suitable because of the lack of statistical analysis of the data.

### *Demonstrations*

When we teach by demonstration, we show a person how to do something or we show the value of an idea, a demonstration is so obvious; it is there before your eyes. It can be applied to local needs and problem. Example is better than precept, showing is better than telling.

### *Types*

*The Method Demonstration.* This is one of the oldest forms of teaching, used by parents with children to teach the skills of hunting, cultivating, building, cooking and so on. You show how to do a job step by step, e.g., baking bread, building a latrine, teaching a class, etc.

*The Result Demonstration.* This shows, after a period of time, the value of an improved practice, e.g. the use of fertilizer, the use of various teaching methods, anti-malarial measures, etc. The result demonstration helps to convince people about a new idea and 'Comparison' is the essential ingredient.

*Method Demonstration.* An extension work is called on to teach villagers how to do many new kinds of work. While showing audience how to do work by doing it himself, he is conducting a method demonstration.

It is a relatively short-term demonstration given before a group to show how to carry out an entirely new practice over older one in a better way.

The method demonstration is given by the extension worker himself or a trained leader or the purpose of teaching a skill to a group.

***Objectives***

To enable the people acquire new skills, to enable people improve their old skill, to make the learners think more efficiently by getting rid of defective practices, to save time, labour and to increase satisfaction of learners, to give confidence to the people that a particular recommended practice is a practicable proposition in their own situation.

***Steps to Demonstrate***

*Analyze the Situation.* To determine the subject-matter, the suitability of visual presentation to a group the possibility of repeating the demonstration by local leaders, the importance of the subject from the farmers viewpoint and the availability of infrastructural facilities.

*Elaborate Demonstration.* Gather all the information about the practice, familiarise yourself with the subject matter. Check on research findings, talk over the problem with a few village leaders, let the villagers help you plan the demonstration and provide land and other requisites, have a time-table, depending on how much skill is required and how soon it is to be acquired, have a job break ups or a demonstration outline giving the operations in logical steps, indentify the key-points, list out the select demonstration materials, arrange for diagrams, directions and other teaching materials to be distributed, prepare kits of special materials needed by local leaders if they are to repeat the demonstration and make sure that the work place is properly arranged.

*Presentation.* Information about the place and time should be given at an early to check-up equipment and material, make proper physical arrangements, explain the purpose and its applicability to the local problem, show each operation slowly, step by step, make sure that the audience can see and hear clearly, emphasize key points, solicit question at each step before going on to the next, give an opportunity to learners to practice the skill, and distribute supplemental teaching material pertaining to the demonstrations.

*Follow-up.* Make publicity and the demonstrations through press, radio, etc., make a sample check to assess the extent of the use of the skill and satisfaction derived.

***Advantages***

Seeing, hearing, discussing and participating in a group stimulate interest and action, the costly trial and error procedure is eliminated, acquirement of skills is speeded, simple demonstrations readily lend themselves to repeated use by local learners, introduces change of practice at a low cost and provides publicity material.

***Limitations***

Suitable only for practices involving skills, needs good deal of preparations, equipment and skill on the part of extension worker, may require considerable equipment to be transported to the work place, requires a certain amount of showmanship, which is not possessed by some extension workers.

***The Result Demonstration***

The result demonstration is a method of teaching to show by example the practical application or an established fact, or group of related facts. In other words, it is a way of showing people the value of an improved practice whose success has already been established on the research station, or laboratory situation followed by district trials or observation plots.

***Objectives of Result Demonstration***

To show the utility and feasibility of a recommended practice under specified conditions, to establish confidence on the part of the learners and home workers as well as the extension workers.

***Procedure to be followed***

*Analyze situation and determine need.* Analyze the need to establish further confidence in local application of research findings and results of observation, understand the experience of the extension worker in guiding and carrying out the practice under similar conditions.

*Decide upon specific purpose.* The audience to whom the demonstration to be carried out, specify what do they want to learn, whether to train the extension worker, or to establish the confidence on the learners.

*Plan the result demonstration.* Consult subject matter specialist; make as simple and clear-cut as possible; decide upon evidence needed and how local proof will be established; determine the number of demonstrations needed to accomplish purpose; locate sources of need materials, collect material and decide place of demonstration.

*Select demonstrators.* Consult with local leaders and select a demonstrator who is interested in improving his practice, visit the prospective demonstrator to make sure that all conditions for success of demonstration are favourable, the demonstrator should be conscious of his responsibility for the successful completion of the demonstration, the demonstrator should be willing for the demonstration to be used for teaching purposes and publicity. The demonstrator should have to secure the necessary equipment supplies and materials to carry out the demonstration to a successful completion, explain and agree upon procedure with demonstrator and leave written instructions.

*Selection of the plot.* The plot or the theme should be representative, and relevant.

*Commencement of the demonstration.* Wide publicity should be given before demonstration. All the material should be kept ready. Should begin the demonstration in the presence of the villagers, home-makers or learners. Make demonstration as clear as possible to all the audience.

*Supervision of demonstration.* Visit the demonstration plot frequently to maintain demonstrators interest, check on progress and see that succeeding steps are performed as outlined, maintain records and assist the demonstrator also keep proper records, publicity should be given to the demonstration through mass media like radio, TV and newspaper, conduct tours to successful demonstration at proper times, care should be taken to be demonstration is completed on specified time.

*Follow-up.* Wide publicity should be given to results of demonstration. Demonstrator should be encouraged to report at meetings, visual aids to be prepared based on the results of demonstration.

### *Advantages of Demonstration*

It provides practical knowledge, it increases confidence of learners in extension worker, it is useful in introducing a new practice. It contributes to discover local leaders. It provides teaching material for further use by extension worker.

### *Limitation*

It requires a lot of time and preparation on the part of the extension worker. It is a costly teaching method. It is difficult to find good demonstrator who will keep records. It may become difficult due to unfavourable weather and other factors. Unsuccessful demonstrations may undermine the prestige of extension and entail loss of confidence.

## General Meetings

The term 'General Meetings' includes all kinds of meetings held by extension workers. There is a large variety of such meetings. In size they run from the small committee/meetings to those held on special occasions. Geographically, the meetings may be held in a neighbourhood, a community hall or village, a block, a district or state. The meetings may be held periodically or occasionally. The method of presentation may be the lecture of formal talk, informal or formal discussion, or of slide show or a motion picture film, steps in conducting the meeting. There are three major steps that could be followed:

1. Planning, 2. Execution, and 3. Follow-up.

### *Plan in Advance for Meeting*

Number of meetings, places and tentative, dates should be

determined; time and place should be selected depending on the season or the year, day of week, and time of day in terms of the work cycles of those persons expected to attend. Select a tentative date and check to see that there are no important competing events that will effect attendance. Select meeting place suitable lighting, ventilation, seating arrangement and other necessary facilities. Encourage participation of local leaders in arranging and conducting the programme. Outline a tentative programme or agenda. As far as possible, hold day time meetings, and reduce meetings in night. Secure speakers or resource persons as needed. Inform speakers regarding local conditions and suggest subject matter be adapted to the needs of local audience. Select the audio-visual aids best suited to the occasion. Provide for social and recreational features. Utilise the methods of publicising the meeting that are necessary to ensure satisfactory attendance of those people the meeting is intended to reach.

### *Conducting the Meeting or Execution*

Start the meeting on time. State the purpose or the objectives and programme of the meeting. Introduction should be brief. Focus attention on central theme. Keep meeting moving on as per the schedule. Use appropriate audio-visual material to explain the content. Watch the reaction of audience and encourage audience participation when desirable. Take action on matters calling for decision at appropriate time. Take advantage of group psychology and employ appeal that arouse interest, create desire and stimulate action. Close meeting on time with brief summary by chairman. Give recognition to individuals and groups that have actively participated, distribute relevant folders or pamphlets at the time of the meeting. Take names of those who are interested in further information or follow-up.

### *Follow-up*

Evaluate the use and procedures of the meeting give publicity to what happened in the meeting in newspapers, radio broadcasts and make farm or home visits, or send additional information to persons requesting for it, and make sample check to determine satisfaction with meeting and the extent to which the information is being used.

### *Advantages of Meetings*

Reaches a large number of people can be adopted to practically all field's of subject matter. Recognises basic urge of individuals for social contacts. Group psychology stimulates and motivate the participants to act with conviction. Promotes personal acquintance between extension worker and the learner. Meetings could be of supplement of other extension methods. Has publicity value and changes could be brought out in practice at low cost.

### *Limitations*

*1. Suitable place.* Suitable place meet and facilities may not be always available. Wide diversity in character and interests of audience may create a difficult teaching situation; may require undue amount of work and preparation on the part of extension worker. Circumstances beyond the control of the learners such as conflicting attractions, unfavourable weather, etc. may result in poor attendance. Meetings which are poorly arranged or conducted may have far-reaching unfavourable effects and if care is not taken the holding of meeting may become the 'real' objective, rather than the purpose the meeting was interested to advance.

*2. Lecture.* The lecture method is extensively used to present authoritative or technical information to develop background and appreciation and to integrate ideas. The range of subjects that can be covered by this method is unlimited. But the speaker at given meeting present a specific subject to a particular audience. The lecture is an excellent method for presenting information to a large number of audience in a short period of time. Its weakness is that people are not likely to assume, because for the most part it is a one-way communication. Members of audience listen in terms of their interest and remember in terms of motivation and memory.

The chief characteristics of the 'lecture method' are usually it is an organised presentation. It can be used to cover thoroughly the subject matter. It is adaptable to large groups. It appeals to the 'ear-minded'. It conserves time, results are easy to check, listeners sometimes absorb information without thinking or reasoning. Material gained through lecture is not really learned and the lecturer may 'lose' his group or go over the heads of his group.

*How to make and when to use Lecture Method.* When there are large groups, individuals have some common background of information and experience; when it is necessary to cover a large quantity of material in a given time; when it is necessary to motivate the audience to initiate a new programme or in further development of a programme; when giving factual information; when providing a common background of information as a basis for further study; and when there is need to supplement other methods.

*The Lecture Method is effective.* When skills are to be developed, no testing is done, group participation is desired, problems are to be solved, and 'doing' ability is to be acquired.

*3. Debate.* The common pattern is to have two teams, one representing the affirmative, and the other the negative side of the question. Usually there are two speakers for each side. Each speaker is allowed a definite amount of time to make his main speech and rebuttal after the main speeches have been completed.

Debate is two-way communication between the debaters, but one-way communication for the audience. The range of subjects for debate is limited to controversial topics. The big advantages in a debate is that more than one side of a question is presented. If it is a decision debate, there is the temptation for the debate to become highly antagonistic. In such a case, the motive to win the debate by any means may lead to distortion of information, ignoring the primary need to inform the audience. This objection to the debate is overcome by holding non-decision debates, or by having a forum after the debate.

*4. Symposium.* This is a short series of lectures on a specific theme usually by 2 to 5 speakers. Each one speaks for a definite time period and presents a different phase or subdivision of a general topic. The topic should be large enough or general enough to permit two or more subdivisions that are sufficiently significant to justify separate discussion by speakers. The subject may not be controversial. It is important that the speakers are of approximately equal ability, to avoid one speaker dominating the meeting or giving the audience a distored view of the subject. The speech may be followed by a forum to facilitate mastery of information. The advantage of symposium over lecture is that two or more experts present different phases of the topic. It also has an advantage over the debate as it is possible to escape the antagonism that may accompany the latter.

*5. Panel Discussion.* It is an informal conversation put on for the benefit of the audience, by a small group of speakers, usually from 2 to 8 in number. They are selected on the basis of the information and experience they have. Members are seated so that they can see one another and also face the audience. The panel is generally rehearsed before it is presented to the public. The leader introduces the members of the panel to the audience and announces the topic. He has the responsibility to see that the conversation keeps going, by asking questions or making brief comments and encouraging the less talkative members.

***Types of Panel***

- (a) *The question-answer panel.* Here the presentation is actually a series of questions by the leader and answers by the members.
- (b) *Set-speech panel.* Here, each one makes a prepared speech.
- (c) *The conversational panel.* Here, the members hold a conversation among themselves on the topic, with questions and comments going from one member to another.

The third type is more nearly in line with the definition of a panel than the other two, and is the pattern to be achieved.

*6. Buzz Sessions.* With large groups, when there is limited time for discussion, the audience may be divided into smaller units for a short period. This is called, "Buzz Session" or "Huddle System". Groups of 6 to 8 persons get together after receiving instructions to discuss a specific issue assigned. The secretary of each small group will report the findings. It is actually a device to get more people. It participate in a forum.

*7. Brain Storming.* It is a type of small group interaction designed to encourage the free introduction of ideas of an unrestricted basis and without any limitations to feasibility. It is a form of thinking in which judicious reasoning gives way to creative initiative. Participants are encouraged to list for a period of time all the ideas that come to their minds regarding some problem and are asked not to judge the outcome. At a later period all the contributions will be sorted out, evaluated and perhaps later adopted.

*8. Workshop.* It is essentially a long meeting from one day to several weeks, involving all the delegates in which the problems being discussed are considered by delegates in small private groups. There must be a planning session where all are involved in the beginning. There must be considerable time for working sessions, working followed up summarising and evaluation sessions at the close. The workshop as the name implies must produce something in the end a report, a publication, a visual any other material objects.

*9. Seminar.* It is one of the most important forms of group discussion. The discussion leader introduces the topic to be discussed. Members of the audience discuss the subject to which ready answers are not available. A seminar may have two or more plenary sessions. This method has the advantage of pooling together the opinions of a large number of persons.

*10. Conference.* It is a form of discussion method wherein a large number of audience participate and discuss about an issue or a theme. Pooling of experiences and opinions of a group of people who have special qualifications in an area is the main concern. Some action plan or resolutions are drawn at the conclusion of the conference to be presented to any organisation or a body.

### *Advantages of Group Contact Method*

The method helps in deciding debatable issues; fairly large number of audience can be reached; group planning and group action could emerge; some solutions group interests and problems are discovered for arriving at participants share the pride of having helped to solve the problem. It helps develop objectivity towards ideas and sympathetic attitude towards those who disagree.

### *Limitations*

Sometime it is difficult to arrange and manage large gathering factions in the village or among the participants might hinder the effective working of the method. Conclusions and solutions while discussing there is possibility of creating rivalries and thus arrive at same.

### *Mass Contact Methods*

In addition to the personal contact methods and the face-to-face group methods, mass media enable extension workers to greatly increase their teaching efficiency. Publications, newspaper articles, circular letters, radio, television exhibits, posters, etc. provide helpful repetition for those contacted personally or through groups. They also facilitate dissemination of information to a much larger and different clients. Even though the intensity or effectiveness of the reaching contact through mass media is less. The large number of people reached at the low cost per unit of coverage. The extension teaching plan which neglects the communication possible through mass media fails to fully capitalise on what has already been invested in the more intensive contact methods.

### *Circular Letter*

Circular letter is a letter reproduced and sent to many people by the extension worker, to publicise success of an extension activity or to give timely information of farm and home problems.

### *Purposes*

To call the clients to attend a meeting, to stimulate interest in a subject and motivate, to adopt a new practice, to perform a service to community or block, to answer a questionnaire to maintain interest and co-operation of youth club members, local leaders, co-operators, etc. and to take immediate action prevent spread of pests and diseases.

### *Procedure and Principles*

Determine the role of the circular letter in the teaching plan, determine specific purpose of the circular letter and the segment of extension clientele to be reached.

### *Plan the Use of the Circular Letter*

Letter should serve definite purpose, should be important, timely, and related to specific needs and interests, indicate for each subject-matter the number of letters, nature of contents, and approximate date of distribution, organise letters on a series basis, when desirable and check duplicating and mailing equipment in advance so that you do not waste time.

### *Write Circular Letters and Get Them Duplicated*

Appeal immediately to personal interest with a snappy statement in the first paragraph, pointing out the importance of the problem to the person addressed, give a cartoon or illustration containing the central idea. Have a single purpose; state the facts concerning the nature or seriousness of the problem; suggest what the person can do to alleviate or solve the problem; letter must be neat and appealing to the eye, and free from errors.

### *Above All, Personalise Your Letter by Using*

Expressions you use in everyday contact, direct statements, simple sentences, action words with few affixes personal references, appropriate anecdotes and courteous conclusion.

### *Advantages*

In addition to the advantages given in the case of 'publications', the following are the special advantages of writing circular letters.

It conveys timely information effectively to special interest groups, it is suited to make announcements to get attendance, circular letters have the advantage of making more direct appeal, than news items or announcements, especially helpful in maintaining interest and co-operation of local leaders, demonstrators or co-operators and the author's enthusiasm and personality can put life into the information carried in such letters.

### *Limitations*

Special equipment and more clerical help are necessary, too frequent use may minimise effectiveness, if clientele are illiterate it is not suitable, and does not have the advantage of personal letters in catering to the needs of a particular individual.

### *News Items and Articles*

News is timely information that interests a number of persons, and the best news is that which has the greatest coverage of the greatest number. It should be an accurate, unbiased account of the main facts of a current event that is of interest to the readers of a newspaper.

### *Purposes*

To inform general public certain news items, to disseminate subject matter information, to create favourable attitude and interest, to reinforce other extension methods like meetings and demonstrations.

*Technique*

***1. Remember that news should have one or more of the following characteristics:***

Something that actually happens, unusual, important, near to the point of publication or audience, new, recent or timely, something that interests clients, catastrophe, fight, conflict, struggle, e.g., competing for a prize in fruit show new knowledge.

2. ***Principles of Good Reporting:***

Write the lead sentence which tells the crux of the situation, use the pyramid form of writing, use the five W's and one H as guide, i.e., see, if you have answered the who, what, why, when, where and how, get as many of these as possible in the first paragraph as a self-guard against editor's cutting, use in simple language, avoid using your personal opinion, be accurate, fair and brief, include motivating appeals, evaluate effectiveness of news articles.

*Advantages*

(a) Low cost.

(b) Large coverage in short-time.

(c) Efficient source of timely information.

(d) Carries the prestige and confidence of the printed word.

(e) Reinforcing effect on other extension methods.

(f) Tax payers come to know about extension activities (public relations).

*Limitations*

(a) It is of no value if people are illiterate or do not read or hear newspaper.

(b) It is difficult to check the results.

(c) It requires special training to write good articles.

## Publications

*General Purpose*

The purpose of writing is to communicate certain news. Therefore the first consideration must be the reader. If there are writing for a scientific paper, we have to use a vocabulary and style different from what we would use when writing for the general public

### *Principles*

How clearly you communicate information to average readers depends on how will you select, organize and sort your facts.

**1. *Select Facts***

(a) *Suitable subject matter.* Does it meet a need? Is it timely? Is it current interest? Does it apply to your area? Is information practical?

(b) *Readers.* Who are the people your want to reach? What are their problems, interests and educational levels? Do they have the environment and capacity to make use of the information.

(c) *Purpose of publication.* What do you want to teach and accomplish? Do you want to stimulate interest in a programme, do you want to influence the people to do something?

**2. *Organise Facts***

(a) Shift essential facts necessary to give information clearly.

(b) Screen our difficult concepts which are beyond readers experience or understanding.

(c) Give layman an appreciation of subject rather than a detailed explanation.

(d) Express highlights.

(e) Don't try to impress the layreader with all you know.

(f) Don't document everything.

**3. *Sort Facts***

(a) Arrange facts in logical order.

(b) Set out important points in 1, 2, 3 orders.

(c) Guide reader with attractive subheads and suitable illustrations and pictures.

**4. *Remember the ABC's of journalism***

Accuracy, brevity and clarity; which are the fundamentals of all good writing.

***5. Tips for readability***

(a) Short sentences, clear in meaning, simple in construction with few prepositional phrases and dependent clauses. Give an idea in each sentence.

(b) Simple words—familiar, concrete words.

(c) Personal, or human-interest words.

***Advantages***

It can reach a large number of people quickly and simultaneously. It can be read at leisure, and kept for further reference. Generally people have confidence in the printed page. Necessary supplement to other teaching methods. Informations are usually definite, well-organised and readily understood. Influences adoption of practices at relatively low cost. Provides scope for recognising achievements of individuals and groups. May promote literacy.

***Limitations***

1. Not suited for illiterate audience.
2. Frequent revision may be necessary to keep abreast of current research.
3. Information prepared for general distribution may not fit local conditions.
4. Impersonal, lacks social value of personal contacts and meetings.

***Exhibitions***

Exhibition is one of the best programmes of extension which the extension wings or extension workers can arrange successfully. An exhibition can show actual things, practices, results of demonstrations, programmes in progress through charts, diagrams, displays, layouts models, etc. for village meetings.

***Exhibitions in villages on a small scale***

For arranging exhibitions in villages, the extension wings may have their own charts, diagrams, models, purchased or prepared or in the extensions, wings. Some of the things can be borrowed from sections of the college or from sections of research or extension.

### *Display*

Exhibits should be displayed and planned so as to be easily seen. Photographs, charts and posters should be prominently placed, at eye-level.

### *Material for stands, etc.*

As far as possible use material available in the villages, stands of bamboo or wood, woven with *newer*, *kana*, *chatai*, *sutli*, etc., may be prepared for permanent use. Card-board folders or folders of plywood or hard board, may also be prepared. Even *charpais* arranged in a U-shape can serve this purpose.

### *Framing*

For framing, we can paste pictures on card-board and put bamboo or wooden frames. Frames which are replaceable with catches at the back can be made. The pictures or diagrams may be framed in glass and put in wooden crates, so that they are not damaged in transport.

### *Exhibits specimen and models*

Good exhibits tells a story without the need of an attendant while planning to prepare an exhibit, limit it to one idea and make it simple and large. It should be timely durable and attractive having bold letters and few times. All parts which need explanation should be labelled.

### *Campaign*

Campaign is an intensive teaching activity undertaken at an opportune time for a brief period, focussing attention in a concerted manner on a particular problem, with a view to stimulate the widest possible interest in a community, block or other geographical area. Campaigns are launched only after a recommended practice has been found acceptable to the people as a result of other extension methods like method or result demonstrations, etc.

### *Purpose*

The objective of campaign is to encourage emotional participation of a large number of people, and to foster a favourable psychological climate for quick and large-scale adoption of an improved practice.

### *Procedure*

Determine the need for a campaign. Be clear about the purpose. Make sure that it fulfills the need of local people.

### *Planning of the Campaign*

Consult local leaders and organizations, consult specialists. Ensure timely supply of men and materials. Select a suitable time for launching the campaign, give wide publicity in advance, build up enthusiasm of the people. Allot specific areas and items to each service personnel and local leaders.

### *How to Conduct the Campaign?*

(a) Ensure that campaign is carried out as per plan.
(b) Work with and through local leaders.
(c) Watch the campaign closely throughout.
(d) Avoid failures.

### *Follow up*

(a) Make individual and group contacts to find out reactions.
(b) Assess extent of adoption.
(c) Find out and analyse failures.
(d) Publicise successful items.
(e) Give due recognition to local leaders responsible for success.

### *Advantages*

1. Specially suited to stimulate mass scale adoption of an improved practice in the shortest time possible.
2. Facilitates exploitation of group psychology for introducing new practices.
3. Successful campaigns create conductive atmosphere for popularising other methods.
4. Builds up community confidence.
5. This method is of special advantage in the case of certain practices which are effective only when the entire community adopts them.

### *Limitations*

1. Applicable to only a few of topics of common interest, but not suited to solve individual problems.

2. Successful only when all participants co-operate in the campaign.
3. Not useful when advocated practice involves complicated technicalities.
4. Requires adequate preparation and close association of officials and non-officials, concerted efforts and propaganda techniques.

### *Radio*

Radio is a medium for communication—a tool for giving information and entertainment. Low cost radios and transistors are available in the market. Hence there is a shift even among the poor from community listening to individual listening at home.

### *Purposes*

To reach large number of people quickly and inexpensively, to reach people not reached by other means, and media, to stimulate participation in extension through all other media, to build enthusiasm and maintain interest.

### *Procedure*

Determine its place in the teaching plan. Be clear about the purpose of your broadcast; keep the interests and needs of the audience in view; select topics of current interest, time the broadcast to synchronise with the client's leisure hours; decide what method to be followed straight talk, interview, panel discussion, drama, etc., for writing the script, follow the principles given for writing news articles, encourage people to listen to rural programmes, encourage them to write to the boadcasting stations about their likes, needs and opinions, encourage talented local people to participate in broadcasting.

### *Advantages*

Can reach more people quickly than any other means of communication, specially suited to give emergency and timely information, relatively cheap, reaches people who are unable to attend extension meetings, a means of informing non-farm people about agricultural matters, builds interest in other extension media, possible to do other things while listening.

***Limitations***

Limited number of boadcasting stations, not within reach of all farmers, recommendations may not apply to individual needs, no turning back if not understood, frequently loses out in competition with entertainment, difficult to check on results.

***Television (TV)***

Television is one of the important mass media for dissemination of information in the rural areas.

Television has unique advantages over other mass media, while it provides words with pictures and sound effects like the movies, it cores over the latter by its high intimacy and reaches the largest number of people at the shortest possible time. The TV-viewing has the advantage over the radio. Television can deal with topical problems, and depict known persons who can provide the solutions. People learn through the eye, and will remember things better if they see them. Television-viewing does not demand the strain and discipline needed to read the printed medium. The messages on the TV screen are pre-selected, sorted out and then presented in the simplest manner possible.

Demonstrations, "the need" in extension education are brought to the learner by television. This has great value in making converts to better practices.

Experience both in India and in other countries shows that it has limitations. As a mass medium, TV programme lead to awareness, contribute information and perhaps help form opinion. Before the farmer thinks of taking action, he will require the televised information and impression to be reinforced by local demonstration and individual personal conformation.

Television everywhere is concentrated very strongly with the first stage of awareness. It is strong in providing a stimulus and exposing the audience to a whole of ideas and experiences.

***Entertainment First***

The main motive behind viewing television is to get entertainment in its widest sense, and not with a purpose of learning something. Entertainment includes everything which is pleasant, contains good humour and which indirectly provides a lot of interest in the idea presented. This calls for a good showmanship.

Among these factors, timing, frequency, and length, format or design, content and the treatment used for putting the content across are the most important ones.

### *Timing*

So far as timing is concerned we know what time of evening is the most suited for viewing. However, radio listening surveys have shown that the evening time is the most unsuitable time for housewives to listen to and the most suitable time for them, when they are free of the household chores, is the afternoon. This has to be taken into consideration while planning special programmes for women.

### *Frequency and Length*

Depending upon the programme and its content, it may take anywhere between eight hours and several months to produce a half-an-hour programme. Unlike for the radio, it would be impossible to produce a quality programme at short notice in television. The frequency of the programme will, therefore, depend entirely on the manpower, equipment and funds available. A programme twice a week at least in the initial years of TV should be more than ample.

### *Format*

There are two alternatives available to TV for the format of the programme, depending upon content and purpose. First where the programme is on one single message or subject considerable research and planning will be needed. The second type contains two or more short items, each item by itself complete, which then will take the form of a magazine. Hence, such items should also be carefully produced giving time sufficient enough for understanding and absorption in the rural mind.

### *Content*

The content of the programme has to serve and has to satisfy the dual purpose of information and entertainment. The broadcaster himself needs to use his talent in showmanship to combine all the ingredients of the programmes and present it in a pleasant manner to the audience.

### *Treatment*

Treatment is related to content. But whatever the content, what is expected is a good quality not only in the visuals but also in sound.

There is one important aspect of visuals which is yet to be fully explored in India, i.e. the use of still photographs. These are much easier to operate, faster to get results from and can be used very effectively where motion is not vital to the programmes. Photographs offer us package of programmes which can be very good stand-bys. Extensive libraries of such packages could be built up in the TV studios, and produced and supplied by agricultural research and development organizations.

### *Research Before Production*

It is essential to find out the requirements and the opinion of the people about the programme research in programming is an important factor which has unfortunately not been given enough attention. Lack of research results in the facts tending to disappear and errors.

### *Need for Rehearsals*

Like research preceding a programme rehearsal is a very important aspect of telecasting. It will give a good idea of what to avoid, what to introduce in the programme. Rehearsals, therefore, should invariably precede actual telecasting. When talks are scheduled, it is necessary that they are accompanied by the use of film or stills, and if possible also by studio demonstrations.

### *Personnel*

Probably the TV commentator would be the one that has to appear the most. It is his personaiity that has gone to be liked by the viewer and this has, in turn, great influence on him in establishing the relationship between himself and what is said and shown on TV.

### *Indigenous Methods*

Indigenous methods makes use of the naturally available resources within the community for its extension teaching programmes.

### *Puppets*

Usually as in drama the learners make an imagination and immediate response to puppets. Puppets can be interesting aids for telling some stories ideas to the people. Puppets are the best means of instruction especially to the illustrators. Any type of characters, i.e. even the animals and birds can be presented, for a wide variety of subjects.

### *Making Puppets*

Bottom of the paper bags can be cut into different figures and used or faces or figures in the old newspapers or pictures can be cut and pasted.

Glove puppets can be made out of old cloth, paper mache, paper, and glove. Faces can be made using paper mache or pieces of papers pasted one after another. Glass leads can be used from eyes, eyebrows and lips can be painted.

### *Stage*

Any type of arrangements can be made to stage the show. Blanket, sheet or saree can be spread across a door or between two pillars.

Table put on its side can become a screen. Two chairs or trees or twings can be placed appart and a blanket or sheet can be used as screen.

A resourceful person will easily make his theatre for a puppet show. Good lighting is essential and the lights should be directed towards the puppets not towards the audience.

### *Script for Puppet Play*

Any theme relevant to the learners can be chosen. The theme should have dramatic value. The lesson should be direct and clear result of an incident.

Only one idea at a time should be presented. The characters should be distinctive and strong so that they will have strong appeal. The situations should be familiar to the audience. There can be a maximum of two puppeteers for four characters on the stage otherwise there may be confusion.

Action is important in puppet show, than narrative or speech. so there should be short speeches and no silent pauses. There can be of more humour and wits, songs, music and dance to attract the audience's attention.

We can make the puppets to converse with the audience also besides having conversations among themselves. Someone for the audience can answer the questions asked by the puppets in order to make sure that the audience are following the theme and be allert. The wile make the audience to be the participant in the learning process.

### *Glove or Hand Puppets*

Glove or hand puppet is simple to prepare some stories which can be shown with the help of such puppets. These puppets can also be prepared in the class or on different themes by both teachers and learners.

Glove puppet is like a three-fingered glove, which fits in the hand. The first finger is inserted inside the head and moves it when we tell a story. The middle finger and thumb fit in the hands and move them. The dress covers the hand and forearm. One person can operate two puppets at a time, one on either hand.

### *Drama*

Drama is not only another form of entertainment, but it can be an enriching experience for both the audience and the performers, the learners and the teachers. There are many types of drama such as mime, dance, drama, table air, charade, play, pageant, liturgical drama, shadow play, epic and role play.

Formal drama needs written script rehearsals and then enacting. Whereas in prompt dramatization, the story and the situations are suggested and people make up actions and use their own words as dialogue. Participants or the audience themselves can act provided they are motivated properly especially those who cannot read.

Drama is an active method of learning with high degree of participation. The people who watch become emotionally unvalued with the characters in the drama and the message can easily be communicated, as it communicates through feelings and emotions to the audience. Any issue relating to education, health, nutrition, social problems can be easily communicated to the people. Thus drama becomes an effective media of extension work to the people who are interested in dissemination of ideas to the learners.

### *Folk Songs and Folk Dances*

The villagers have a great fascination for their folk songs and dances. We go closer to them if we participate with them and organize such functions, at times of exhibitions, meetings, film-shows, drama, etc. Song connected with the developed programmes and practices in local dialects can be composed by some students or villagers and sung with the help of Harmonium. Tabla, Sarangi, Jhanj, Chitam, etc. This is a good way of conveying the information to the villagers. We can arrange competitions for songs and dances and can give even some prizes if possible. The block staff has some funds for such programmes.

# 7

# COMMUNICATION

Communication is an integral part of sharing information or imparting education. It is an essential process of social life. Throughout age, communication has served to bring man and man together, has helped him to understand his fellow being and to sense the feeling of oneness, which is the basis of social life. Without communication no transmission of information is possible. The message that gets no response is not communication. An effective communicator makes even the complex issues as simple and clear to the audience, communication should be a two-way process.

## Definition of Communication

The word communication has been derived from the Latin word *communis* which can be translated as common. However, communication incorporates, besides commonalty, the concepts of transfer, meaning and information. The communication can be defined as the process through which two or more persons come to exchange ideas and understanding among themselves.

Communication, as defined by Leagens, "is the process by which two or more people exchange ideas, facts, feelings or impressions in ways that each gains a common understanding of the meaning, intent, and use of the messages".

Communication can occur even without words. Psychologists have proved that body movements correlate to feelings. For instance, it is said that if a person touches his nose or ear every 30 seconds, he is a liar. This kind of body language is scientifically called 'Kinesics'. Earlier man used only kinesics to communicate with his fellow beings. Hence, it is just not a wonder that the process of communication has a long history to look back.

Well, before trying to learn the various theories behind the process of communication, let us have a small recreation. Have you heard of the famous Russian Queen Maria Fyodorovna? She was the wife of King Czar Alexander III. She once tried to save the life of a man sentenced to death, the original death warrant written and communicated by her husband was; "pardon impossible, to be sent to Siberia". This communication was cleverly changed by Maria by transposing a single comma. Now Czar's instruction was read as follows: "Pardon, impossible to be sent to Siberia". The prisoner was set free. So, every word, every symbol, gesture and even the punctuation marks (as in the above case) carry meaning and they play an important role in communication process.

## Nature of Communication

According to the situation and structural variations in the communication process, nature of communication may be classified as follows :

| | |
|---|---|
| Inform | : Factual information. |
| Educate | : 'A' and 'B' learn through interaction. |
| Entertain | : The technique of presentation is followed in each way to create interest. |
| Emotionalise | : The participant is made to dissatisfy with the present and an urge is created to move. |
| Persuade | : Suggest new ways to try out even the cost of risk or expense, if any. |
| Reinforce | : Suggested measures are found successful and rewarding. Encourages strengthening of newly followed practices. |

### *Development of Communication Theory*

Although the study of human communication has had a long tradition, the years following World War I, saw the beginning of a rising tide of interest in the study of communication.

During the 1950s, dissidents within the established

departments who were primarily interested in oral communication gathered together to form a national association, and shortly thereafter a number of new departments of public speaking were established. Searching for ways to do research and develop theory, some turned to traditional studies of rhetorical history and theory and some developed the scholarly practice of rhetorical criticism, but a substantial number turned to social scientific model and for research methods.

By the 1930s the study of behaviourism and its influence on social sciences was very strong and this made the investigators who wished to study communication, apply the model of behaviourism to their effort. Researchers such as Knower and Hull were involved in this study. Knower studied the effect of emotional and logical-factual arguments on attitudes of college students towards prohibition. He compared both oral and written messages. In 1940, Hull reported the results of his research on the effects of humorous and non-humorous speeches on the attitudes of students towards state medicine.

After World War II the rapid advances by social psychologists and communication scholars in the study of attitude changes resulted in the emergence of an influential school of investigations and theorizing about communication called the attitude change studies. Many social psychologists thereby started to discover the functional relationship (relationship between the communication content, structure and other variables like audience attitude, audience sex, language intensity, etc.) and integrating the relationships mathematically and manipulating them deductively to yield prediction and control.

By the 1950s a number of theorists had put forward explanatory accounts for phenomena more or less directly associated with human communication. Among the first important conceptual schemes for students of human communication were the mathematical theory of communication and consistency or balance explanations of attitude change. In the 1970s widespread effort was under way to critically evaluate philosophical assumptions.

### *Communication Process*

Communication has been defined as a process. The process

is a concept of changing and various elements will be involved in this process. The elements involved are shown in Fig. 7.10.

Sender → Ideas → Encoding → Channel → Receiver → Decoding

Feedback

**Fig. 7.1. The Communication Process.**

Fig. 7.1 shows the following elements in this process :

1. **Sender** : The persons who intends to make contact with the objective of passing information.
2. **Ideas** : The subject-matter of communication. This may be opinion, attitude, views, suggestions, etc.
3. **Encoding** : Since the subject-matter of communication is abstract and intangible, its transmission requires the use of certain symbols such as words, actions, pictures, etc. Conversion of subject-matter into these symbols is the process of encoding.
4. **Channel** : These symbols are transmitted through certain channels, e.g. radio, telephone, air, etc.
5. **Receiver** : Receiver is the person to whom the message is meant for.
6. **Decoding** : Receiver converts the symbols received from the sender to give him the meaning of the message.
7. **Feedback** : Feedback is necessary to ensure that the receiver has received the message and understands it in the same sense as sender wants.

### *Communication Styles and Theories*

Human beings learn to communicate through language, though they have the natural instinct to communicate through gestures.

The word 'style' has a much narrow sense of meaning, which means the distinctive manner of a person—the expression is unique to an individual. The aphorism 'style is the man' points to the: idiosyncratic features of an individual's characteristic mode of communication. How does a communication style came into being? Rhetorical practice furnishes the grounds for a style. A new style begins when small groups of people become disturbed by their here-and-now problems and meet together to discuss their difficulties, or when they associate to play with symbols, or when they communicate to create social bonds.

A new communication style—new word, a new expression—comes into existence when they try to correlate it with some other event that had happened in the past. For example, at times we say, "The ruling party has won a pyrrhic victory in the present election". Is pyrrhic victory a great victory? Certainly not. It is a victory won at a very great price. In other words, you have lost many things or have made many sacrifices in order to gain the victory. How did this expression come about? Phyrrhus was a king who lived in Greece between 319-272 BC. He wanted to expand his kingdom. So, he was always fighting with his neighbours. He also waged a war against the Romans and though he defeated them, he lost more than half of his army in the process. And since Phrrhus lost more than half of his army, any victory gained at a very high price is called a pyrrhic victory. Thus, new words and expressions come into practice when they violate the norms, customs and rules of established styles.

When human beings intervened in the process of communication—communication turned to be an art. Once, they entered the picture and began to systematically change the appearance, shape and form of communication transactions, the process of communication took a new dimension. It become an important subject areas to be investigated and studied. Just think of the art of taste of human beings, once, he started the intake of food, he artfully changed them by baking, basting, boiling, broiling, seasoning, mixing and decorating them. Gradually, he created different styles of cooking and similarly, in the process of communication, he created distinctive styles of communication.

## General Versus Specific Theories of Communication

Theoreticians working to develop a coherent theory to explain a class of communication have tried to distinguish between the general and specific theories of communication. The general theories of communication provide explanations that relate to the way in which people communicate rather than the details of how people communicate in one specific style.

Katz has suggested that one way to develop a general theory about language is to have linguistics make detailed scientific studies of different natural languages such as French and German. With the preliminary descriptive work out of the way, theorists could then make comparative studies and develop a theory composed of features common to a number of languages. In much the same way, scholars might make essentially ethnographic studies to discover the common features shared by a number of rhetorical communities and styles, and such communalities might pave the way to communication theory, similar in scope and generality to the theories of natural sciences.

The special communication theories, are, however, style-specific. They contain the following:

1. Rules of thumb as to how best to create artistic and effective communication transactions.
2. Basic assumptions or values which guide the communication practices, and
3. Descriptions of the examplars of good communication for that community.

### *Special Communication Theories*

Some of the popular styles of communication relate to a limited number of transactional contexts, and then some styles relate primarily to conversation, some to communication on the electronic media, some to negotiating buying and selling agreements and other contracts, some to religious conversion, some to task-oriented group and organizational communication. The following three distinct styles of communication will be examined here. The three styles are commonly known as "public speaking", "interpersonal communications or "relationship communication style" and "the message communication style"

### *Public Speaking Communication Style*

Nineteenth century scholars of communication tended to neglect the communication theory associated with informal transactions and emphasized occasions for oratory in the pulpit, in deliberative assemblies and before the bar. They taught their students rhetories and elocution in order to achieve an examplar of communication which was called eloquence. The public speaking style draws heavily on the rhetorical tradition, going back to classical times for its theoretical developments.

The basic model or examplar of the public speaking style is essentially a situation in which the central character is the speaker. Other parts of the transaction include an audience and an occasion. The speaker is the motivating force in the communication transaction; while taking the occasion into account and adapting to the audience, the speaker sets the whole thing in motion and the audience then responds to whole thing in motion and the audience then responds to the speaker. The speaker selection is furnished a topic and after carefully analysing the audience, the speaker skilfully fashions supporting material to adopt the topic and ideas to the specific audience. The final and most important element in the model is the speech which emerges from the dynamic interplay of the other parts of the model. The audience is not passive but responds moment by moment as the speaker talks and may provide complications to which the speaker must then adapt. The speaker who succeeds against high odds that is, against a hostile audience or on an unfavourable occasion—is generally evaluated as having produced a better speech than one who gains a favourable response under more favourable conditions.

The speaker in this style of communication is alert to the audience's responses and adjusts to the unfolding situation. The speaker succeeds or fails in the process of communication transaction on the basis of their native ability, trained artistry, and the capacity to take initiative and act in such a way that he or she achieves consciously thoughtout objectives and purposes.

A good public speaking communication transaction is one in which a skilful speaker with a clear purpose analyses the audience and occasion carefully and wisely, selects a suitable topic, develops an organizational pattern, fills in the outline with suitable amplifying material, delivers the speech with appropriate non-verbal gestures and vocal intonations.

As the neophyte physicist learns the paradigm of Newtonian mechanics by doing experiments, such as the inclined plane and the pendulum, so the beginning public speaker learns the examplar by giving speeches. The student learns the rules and norms as well as the standards of goods peaking by the process of giving speeches to audiences according to the expectations.

The theory associated with a good public communication transaction is related to the basic parts of the examplar. The theory deals with the communicative behaviours. In addition, the finer points of the theory consider those communications that may or may not be performed. In short, the theory spells out the rules that provide the boundaries of approved speech behaviour within the context as well as the area of freedom within which people can vary tactics. Usually the theory considers contextual rules in terms of types of speeches, the nature of informative speeches and occasions appropriate for such discourse. The theory discusses the nature of the ideal speaker and ways in which neophytes can learn to project an effective figure from the platform. The theory includes generalizations about the nature of audiences and deals with the characteristics of audiences such as socio-economic and educational backgrounds, interest in aptitudes and attitudes.

Since the speech itself is perhaps the most important feature of the examplar of public speaking communication, the theory deals with many aspects of the speech. Individuals should deal with a given area, select a central idea, analyze the collected information in order to find the logical connections which exist among the various subissues, and finally to come to some structured explanation of the main theme. Another aspect of theory, is to organize the material to adopt it to the audience. Such adaptation requires thorough analysis of the characteristics of audience for a given speech. Additional theoretical material will include such things as phrasing the ideas in suitable language and the use of gesture and voice to deliver the speech in an effective way.

### *Relationship Communication Style*

Relationship communication is the most recent of three academic styles emerged in the 1960s. The public speaking and messege communication style emphasize communication as a tool to reach other ends whereas the relationship communication style emphasizes communication as the most important relationship among people, as a positive value in and of itself.

The theorists for the relationship style disliked mathematically expressed formulas, scheme and blue prints. They rejected the model of communication based upon the cybernetic analogy with feedback as a crucial principle for information, transmission and control instruments. They rejected a paradigm that saw human being community like machines.

The theorists for the new style used the term feedback to refer to all the verbal and non-verbal responses that express reaction to another or feelings, or a response to another person's communication behaviour. One of the aphorisms of the style is "You cannot communicate". The point of the principle is that all response to a participant in a communication transaction can be interpreted in terms of relationship, feelings and attitudes.

The principle "You cannot communicate" points up the central rejection of purposive, international communication aimed at control of others in a communication transaction. Unintentional behaviour communicate feelings or atleast others are stimulated to feel and respond and infer meanings from the entire context of communication theorists considerably by the assumption that you cannot communicate. As a result, the theory associated with the relationship style contains much material about non-verbal communication.

The public speaking style devotes considerable theory to the occasions and to the contextual influence on the programmes governning certain transactions within its purview. The relationship communication style features context as part of its concern with non-verbal communication. The theoretical formulations deal with such contextual features of communication transactions as where people sit or stand in relationship to one another, what sorts of clothes they wear, what their hair styles are, how they walk, how they gesture, how close they are to one another when they speak, whether they touch and how they communicate through senses such as touch and smell.

Like the public speaking style, the transactional model of the relationship style is dramatistic, but it features not one central person but several co-operatie participants who cease to play games with one another and who are real and honest, who take risks and disclose their authentic selves. Their basic attitude is that they should deal with others as authentic human beings and not as things or machines. As authentic communicators, they are open and they welcome human relationships. The self-disclosing communication tends to open up others, and they in turn disclose. The emotional tone of the communication is warmed by congruent, honest and open communication as people take more and more risks and are accepted for themselves.

In the warm and trusting climate of a good communication transaction, people can reveal their innermost feelings and discuss their hopes and fears. They can express their feelings, cry and laugh without worry acceptance or rejection. As the climate builds to ever more intimate and significant communication, important relationships evoke among the participants.

One way to build good self-image is by participating in communication according to the standards and norms of the style.

The process of communication, the transactions in which all participate and create meanings, results in the participants discovering their potential and becoming aware of their authentic selves. In the ideal situation the result for the individual is a stronger self-image a greater sensitivity to others.

### *Message Communication Style*

Message communication style is evolved historically after the public speaking style and before the relationship style.

The basic idea of the theory is that of human beings communicating with a machine. Cybernetics is the study of the way human beings set goals and control behaviour to achieve them, and the way machines can come to serve the function. The study of cybernetics is based upon the ability of organisms and machines to provide and use feedback. The term 'feedback' refers to the information about the output of machine or the behaviour of an organism that is continuously feed to a control device and changes the operation or behaviour in order to correct errors and achieve predetermined goals. Feedback in the message communication style is quite different from the concept as used in the relationship style. Feedback in the relationship style is essentially a response of any sort whatsoever and often is evaluative.

Gcod communication transmitted information with high fidelity. That is, the more information the system transmitted from the source to receiver without distortion or loss, the higher the fidelity of transmission and better the communication event. Noise in a communication system cuts down on fidelity and is, therefore, undesirable. To combat noise such as static, it was discovered that repetition of message elements increased a receiver's ability to decipher the appropriate information.

The theorists called this repetition of message elements as redundancy. The examplar of the style, therefore, is one in which noise was minimised and the redundancy level adjusted to a rate that resulted in high-fidelity transmission of information with no unnecessary repetitions.

Fig. 7.2. presents a typical schematic description of the communication transaction in message communication style.

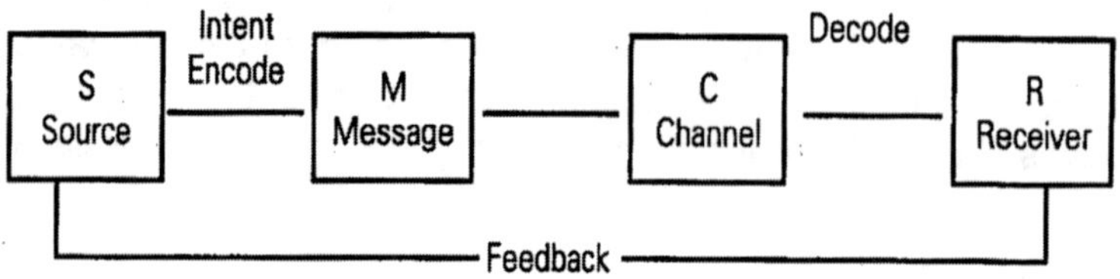


**Fig. 7.2. A typical schematic description of the examplar communication in the message communication style.**

The examplar of the communication style portrays an initiator and controller of the communication transaction in the form of a source. The source begins with a goal for the transaction, encodes messages to achieve the goal, selects proper channels, transmits the message to the receiver, and awaits feedback to discover whether or not the communication was 'successful in achieving the goal. Notice that in the message communication style the concept of feedback is closely related to the motion that the message source has a clear goal against which to test the responses of the receiver.

The instructor will often repeat the exercise using a new pattern in each repetition and increasing the number of channels and the opportunity for feedback from replication to replication. The instructor creates an ever closer approximation of the examplar model of a communication transaction in the message communication style. After each replication the fidelity of information transmission is checked by comparing the replication of the pattern drawn by the receivers with the pattern the source was seeking to get them to replicate.

Human communication exhibits a wide intercultural and historical diversity. Even within the same historical period and culture, various divergent styles of communication came into existence.

### General Theories of Communication

Studies on humanism and the criticisms made on the special theories of communication gave rise to the general theories of communication. To examine more closely how the theorists of humanism and social science generalised the theories of communication, it is essential to examine the ways in which they record their findings. The humanists kept an authentic record of their examinations by performing two important guardian functions, i.e. (i) testing and evaluating the historical traces to establish their authenticity, and (ii) testing and evaluating the evidence contained within the authenticated traces to judge their accuracy and usefulness.

The authentic record consists of the fragments of the past that are useful for the scholar.

Some philosophers of communication have suggested that humanistic and social scientific studies can be brought into fruitful co-operation by using the generalizations of humanists to furnish the hypotheses for social scientists.

To summarize, a total account of human behaviour that explains not only general features of human symbol using but also provides understanding of the details of specific episodes will required both special and general theories, as detailed in the previous chapters. The total account of communication might well include humanistic studies which supplement social scientific investigations to explain how human beings acquire competence in language, in styling communication, in developing rules, and in making choices about strategy and tactics, and indeed about whether or not to conform to communication related conventions.

### *Mass common theories*

Mass communication is an empirical communication to mobilise human resources so as to carry out development messages to the community. In a contemporary world, it will be very difficult to survive if one gets confined to one's own knowledge. Communication is a part of everyone's life. We take some message to the people and if the message had rightly reached them, it produces some effect on the people.

Mass communication has made the quality of the people improve stage by stage. It plays a powerful role in nation-building and development and contributes significantly to bring about social change in the desired direction.

### *Ways of Effective Utilization of Mass Media*

Any medium can be referred to as mass medium not merely because of the numbers. It is the total interactive situation—whether the information given produces change. If medium A produces greater change in the masses than medium B, then medium A is the best medium.

How to make mass media more effective in rural development programmes?

1. In villages let the illiterates also hear the news from the newspaper as it is read by the literates.
2. If there are panchayat TV sets, let it not be in the hands of village heads—let it be made accessible to every people in the village.
3. In case of programmes of instruction, it should be made effective so that it makes people sit and watch the programme.
4. Care should be taken such that the cultural values of people are not exploited to improve the profit of the product.

5. When a message is sent, we should be aware also of the format through which it is sent.
6. The message should reach the mass without any interruption.

As for the general theories of communication process, there are also theories related to mass communication.

***Authoritarian Theory***

Many communist countries are governed by authoritarian principles. In olden days, people thought that people other than those in power were not trustworthy. There was very strict control of the press through licensing. Censorship of press was practised. They could withhold information if they wanted.

The extent or the level of authoritarianism is not the same world over. The degree of authoritarianism differs in different countries.

A broad classification of authoritarianism theory can be made as follows :

1. Complete control of press—this category includes countries such as China and Yugoslavia.
2. Criticisms are theoretically allowed by government and it insists on censorship. Hence the press is handicapped and there is no freedom of expression. This type of press control is found in countries like Columbia, Egypt and Syria.
3. In countries like South Africa, Iran, Pakistan, Iraq and Lebanon, special press laws are framed for the control of press.
4. In Turkey, Afghanistan and Indonesia the press freedom is suppressed.

***Liberatian Theory***

Though the press existed outside the government, all principles, policies, ideologies of the government were popularised, supported and advocated by the press.

People act in an impulsive manner, in authoritarian theory whereas in Liberation theory, the people activate their faculty of reasoning. Reasoning and moral integrity are developed through judgement, self-control, looking into intrinsic values before arriving at any conclusions.

The following are the ways of developing reasoning:

1. By separating right from wrong.
2. Good from bad, and
3. Truth from falsehood.

In democratic countries, the functions of the press are to inform to tell, to entertain and to see Liberatian principles are followed.

***Social Responsibility Theory***

Social Responsibility theory is an outgrowth of the Libertian theory. The 20th century United States is an example for social responsibility theory.

The functions of the press under this theory are given below:

1. To provide information discussion and debate on public affairs.
2. To instruct and inform the public on important issues. Willuer Shram has identified the types for communication under this theory as
   (a) Information
   (b) Instruction
   (c) Persuasion
   (d) Entertainment.

Of these, the mostly preferred form of communication through media is to be an entertainer.

3. The individual has to be protected as he or she may not be able to wage a lone battle against the government because of the limited resources. Hence, the press comes to the rescue of the individual.
4. Maintenance of economic equilibrium brings the buyers and sellers together.
5. Media provides entertainment.
6. Press should remain independent of outside pressure.

### *Soviet Communist Theory*

Soviet Communist theory is an outgrowth of the authoritarian theory. The dress and the government function together. The main purpose of this theory is to ensure success of the Soviet Socialist system. Certain Communist countries follow this principle, which is shaky now.

### *Power of Press Theory*

Under this theory comes the following :

(a) Bullet theory

(b) Hypodermic needle theory

(c) Conveyer belt theory, and

(d) Transportation theory.

The message reaches straight to the people. There are no hurdles in between.

The people are considered to be the targets to be shot at. The people don't question the government. They accept the activities of the Government as it is as it comes from the people in power.

### *Agenda Setting Theory*

The editor makes the news sensational and hence attracts the public. Hence, the press has to be very careful about which information deserves to be in first place and which deserves the least importance.

Thus, the media man, confers the status to the news. Therefore, this theory is also called as "Status Conferal Theory".

### *Marshall Mcluhan's Theory*

Marshall Mcluhan classifies the media into two types as

1. Hot media, and 2. Cool media.

*Hot Media*. There is very little audience concentration in this media. People involvement is also very little. Examples of such media are: radio, photography, motion pictures and print media.

*Cool Media*. In this media there is greater audience participation. Examples of such media are: interpersonal communication, cartoon, TV, etc.

### *Social Categories Theory*

The demographic variables such as sex, age, religion, caste, education, occupation, marital status, etc. influence the psychographic variables such as motivations, anxiety, etc.

An advertisement on car attracts the people belonging to high socio-economic status. The low income people will have less interest.

### *Cultural Norms Theory*

Media influence culture.

A culture is a complete whole consisting of knowledge belief, art, moral, law, custom and any other capability attained by man as a member of the society.

Children are socialized by media today and media also create new value system.

### *Ludenic Theory*

Ludenic theory is also known as play theory. Media is considered to mainly as an entertainer and the pleasure seeking principle of the masses is exploited by the media men to attract the people.

### *Theories of Violence*

*Catharsis Theory.* 'Catharsis' means 'emotional release entertainment provides emotional release. This is more applicable to the peopie in lower economic stratum as upper classes have other kinds of diversion to have relief.

*Aggressive ones.* Films of aggressive actions in the film makes the viewer emotionally aroused and they take sides to the character of the film and try to imitate the hero.

*Reinforcement Theory.* Televised violence reinforce the violent behaviour of the individuals.

### *Importance of Communication for Extension Worker*

The extension worker plays an important role in the extension field. Extension work is not limited to the rural areas alone, but extends to urban side as well, although more emphasis is laid on the development of rural sector. Even in one sector, the nature of work is multipurposive. The extension worker is bound to touch upon all aspects of rural life. He should have a comprehensive understanding of the village people and their problems. He should participate in sorrows and joys of the villagers and must develop a close contact with the village people. He is to win the willing and enthusiastic co-operation of the people and the work is to start with the local felt needs.

### *Extension worker as a Communicator*

The over riding challenge to extension workers is to have ideas useful to an audience, to make their meaning clear, to get them accepted and to motivate people to adopt and practise them. Communication is essential to all human association. One's ability to influence others is closely linked with one's ability to communicate one's ideas. The essence of learning of the meaning of new ideas in relation to recognised problems requires good communication. Good communication does not consist merely of giving orders, but of creating understanding. It does not consist merely of imparting knowledge, but of helping people gain a clear view the meaning of knowledge. Certain ideas behind effective communication, when understood by the extension worker, helps them communicate effectively, some of these are as follows :

### *Communication Process*

Communication is limited by one's concept of the communication process. There are many different ways of using or thinking about communication. Successful communication in programmes of rural development is not a single unit act. It requires a series of unit acts planned to assure effective sequence and integration. It starts with the recognition of needs which new ideas can help meet and proceeds until people have acted upon them. Hence, extension education for community development requires the total act of communicating. Extension educators, therefore, must skilfully combine the unit acts into an integrated whole. For, it is only when this is done that they can influence large numbers of village people to substantially change their behaviour. The way one thinks about communication will influence its quality.

### *Communication is a two-way process*

Communication is a two-way process involving interaction between those who are aspiring to communicate and the receivers. Extension workers must make the audience understand clearly what is to be learned and what it should do about it. Questions and comments by the receiver and observation of his behaviour are good ways to tell if one has really communicated. Direct questioning by the communicator, establishing a friendly environment and a permissive climate are others among the many methods for making communication a two-way process of learning.

### *Should have clear idea of the content*

One must have ideas before one can communicate with others. One must communicate about things that exist, that are real and as the audiences see them. A crucial point to remember is that what a person thinks is true, is true to him. And he will act accordingly until what he thinks true is disproved and the real truth accepted by him. Implied here is the fact that people must be willing to listen negotiate, arbitrate and discuss, so that communication takes place. Not only one should have ideas, but one must also know—how to organize them and present them clearly, forcefully, accurately and adequately.

### *Systematic Use of Symbols*

The system of symbols used to present ideas, objects or concepts must be adequate and used skilfully. Practically all communication, especially that involving complex and abstract ideas is done by the use of symbols becuase of two primary reasons:

(a) The inconvenience, impracticability of impossibility of having real objects always available when one wishes to convey ideas.

(b) Many abstract ideas can hardly be made clear except by the use of symbols. Symbols are meaningful to a person only when he understands what they stand for. For example, the symbols used in statistics or other forms of mathematics mean nothing to him until he understands the object, concept or action they represent.

The basic means of communication is words. But communicators must avoid putting an ocean of words into a drop of thought. Words are usually more effective when supported by other forms of symbols that also communicate, such as the many forms of visual aids. Hence, the effectiveness of extension workers, therefore, is ultimately determined by their skill in manipulating words and other symbols that convey useful ideas.

### *Cultural Values and the Social Organisation*

Cultural values and the social organisation are determinants of communication. These tend to differ from one culture to another and within them. Hence knowledge of ideas and action which the value system will accept, and which it will be likely to reject, along with the channels of communication established by the particular social organisation are essential for effective communication.

### *The environment for communication*

The environment created by the communicator influences his effectiveness. The physical facilities, friendliness, respect for others view, recognition of accomplishment of others, permissiveness and rapport, in general, are all important ingredients of a climate conducive to effective communication.

### *Should follow a pattern*

To make sense, the communication effort must be organized according to some specific form or pattern. Organisation may be informal, as a conversation or a discussion or formal as a speech or lecture.

Other common forms are : a story, a play, a debate, a report, a bulletin, a poster, a panel discussion, etc. Whatever the form chosen, the facts to be presented must be organized so as to enable the audience to gain a unified understanding of the message.

### *Co-operation, participation and involvement are essential to communication*

As pointed out earlier communication is a two-way process. It is just not speaking or writing to another person or persons. The respondent must co-operate in listening and responding. There must be interaction between the individuals involved. Both the communicator and the receiver must be brought into the act. Hence, the listener must work little too. For, it is what he does mentally or physically in the form of reaction to the content presented that he really learns, not what the communicator does. Learning is an active process on the part of the learner. The communicator, then, can talk or act with great skill, but if the mind of the receiver is turned in, elsewhere, what is being said or done really makes no difference unless the respondent is on the same wavelength, the character of what is sent out, hardly governs the communication process.

***Standards of Communication Influence its Success***

Standards of communication have to be with the rules as criteria, established by authority, custom or general use, found to be effective as guides to communication. There are several concepts or standards related to the quality of communication. Four primary standards are as follows :

*Standard of Correctness.* This involves the use of correct words or other symbols, correct logic and correct content or facts.

*Standard of Effectiveness.* This relates to the interaction, understanding, meaning, behavioural changes, achievement of objectives, etc. that result from communication.

*Standard of good taste.* This pertains to the importance, of keeping action, content and method compatible with the social code of the society.

*Standard of social responsibility.* This infers that when one communicates one assumes responsibility for the effect of one's communication on the respondents and the society. No one of these standards alone will provide the basis for evaluating communication. All four standards must be given consideration.

***Evaluation is necessary to Improve communication***

Evaluation is the process of finding out what happened as a result of communication. Communications need to know if their expressions were effective, if they were interpreted correctly and what kinds and amounts of response resulted. This knowledge is necessary as a basis for making changes needed to improve subsequent acts of communication. Such information may be attained either formally or informally. Formal checks may be made through direct questions, conversation and observable reactions with members of the audience. Informal evaluation may be made through the use of surveys in many different forms, attitude tests, information tests, etc. Well, with these suggestions to make the extension worker a good communicator, let us try to distinguish an effective and a poor extension worker in his quality—as a communicator.

## Qualities of a Communicator

1. To bring about changes in the existing system in any field a good communicator knows the following :
   (a) The objectives and specifically define them.
   (b) The audience to whom it is to be communicated its needs, interests, abilities, predispositions.
   (c) The message its content, validity, usefulness, importance.
   (d) Channels that will reach the audience and their usefulness.
   (e) Methods of organizing and treatment of message.
   (f) His/her professional abilities and limitations.
2. He/she is interested in the following :
   (a) The audience and its welfare.
   (b) Message and how it can help people.
   (c) The results of communication and their evaluation.
   (d) The communication process.
   (e) The communication channels, their proper use and limitation.
   (f) How to improve his communication skill.
3. He/she prepares the following:
   (a) A plan for communication—a teaching plan.
   (b) Communication materials and equipments.
   (c) A plan for evaluation of results.
4. He/she has skill in the following:
   (a) Selecting messages.
   (b) Treating messages.
   (c) Expressing messages—verbal and written.
   (d) The selection and use of channels.
   (e) Understanding the audience.
   (f) Collecting evidence of results.

### *Poor Communicators*

Poor communicators are often guilty of one or more of the following.

1. Fail to have ideas to present that are really useful to the audience.
2. Fail to give the complete story and show its relationship to people's problems.
3. Forget that time and energy are needed to absorb the material presented.
4. Feel they are always clearly understood.
5. Refuse to adjust to 'closed' minds.
6. Talk while others are not listening.
7. Go far too ahead of audience understanding.
8. Fail to recognise others viewpoint and develop presentation accordingly.
9. Fail to recognise that communication is a two-way process.
10. Let their own biases over influence the presentation.
11. Fail to see that everyone understands questions brought up for discussions.
12. Fail to provide a permissive atmosphere.
13. Disregard the values, customs, prejudices and habits of people with they attempt to communicate.
14. Fail to start where people are, with respect to knowledge, skill, interest and need.

An effective communicator assumes that his audience is intelligent, that his audience, is or can be made, interested in it. He recognises that what is true in the view of given persons, is true to them. Consequently, he assumes that every one tries to do the right thing as they see it. He tries to view what he is doing from the standpoint of his audience. He recognises that his message must get through. He communicates for clear understanding and desirable action by his audience, for it is only with this achievement that communication is successful.

### *Message or Content*

A message is the information a communicator wishes his audience to receive understand, accept and act upon. Messages, for example, may consist of statements of scientific facts about agriculture, sanitation or nutrition; description of action being taken by individuals, groups or communitees; reasons why certain kinds of action should be taken; or steps necessary in taking given kinds of action. Messages are not precisely the same as the subject matter or technology conveyed. They are rather a generalized idea of what the subject-matter says. A successful communication is one in which the messages are controlled as far as possible.

***Characteristics of good message***

1. In line with the objective to be attained.
2. Clear understandable by the audience.
3. In line with the mental, social, economic and physical capabilities of the audience.
4. Significant—economically, socially or aesthetically to the needs, interests and values of the audience.
5. Specific—no irrelevant material.
6. Simply stated—covering only one point at a time.
7. Accurate—scientifically sound, factual and current.
8. Timely—especially when seasonal factors are important and issues current.
9. Supported by factual material covering both sides of the argument.
10. Appropriate to the channel selected.
11. Appealing and attractive to the audience—having ability immediate use.
12. Applicable—audience can apply recommendation.
13. Adequate—combining principle and practice in effective proportion.
14. Manageable—can be handled by them with high professional skill and communicator within the limits imposed by time.

Applied properly, the foregoing criteria for selecting and sending messages will contribute much to the goodness of the message. Effective communicators use them skilfully. In contrast, poor communicators often do the following:

1. Fail to clearly separate the key message from the supporting content or subject-matter.
2. Fail to prepare and organize their message properly.
3. Use inaccurate or 'fussy' symbols—words, visuals, or real objects—to represent the message.
4. Fail to select messages that are sharply in line with the felt needs of the audience.
5. Fail to present the message objectively—present the material often biased, to support only one side of the proposition.
6. Fail to view the message from the standpoint of the audience.
7. Fail to time the message properly within a presentation or within a total programme.

Good selection and 'packaging' messages are essential so that they have a good chance of being understood, accepted and acted upon when received. This is a crucial step in the communication process. It is one of the six keys to success in efforts to influence people to change their ways of thinking and of doing that lead to social and economic improvement. Messages are the content aspects of educational change that is assumed to be desirable in extension education for community development.

### *Channels of Communication*

A channel may be anything used by a sender of messages to connect him with intended receivers. The crucial point is that he/she must get in contact with the audience. The message must get through. The common channels of communication in the extension situation include meetings, radio, books, bulletins, letters, newspapers, organized tours and personal contacts. But channels are no good without careful direction or use in the right way, at the right time, to do the right job for the right purpose and for the right audience. So, proper selection and use of channels is highly important.

The obstruction that enter channels are called 'noise' which prevent the message from being heard or carried over. 'Noise emerges from a wide range of sources.

1. Failure of a channel to reach the intended audience. For example, meetings—all people may or may not attend. Written material cannot be read by many people.
2. Failure on the part of a communicator to handle channels skilfully.
3. Failure to select channels appropriate to the objective of the communicator. For example, if an objective is to show a certain group of people how to do something—dig a composit pit, cook vegetables etc.,—the radio or newspaper would not do the job instead a demonstration meeting can do it.
4. Failure to use channel in accordance with the ability of the audience: Written materials for example cannot serve as useful channels to communicate information to people who cannot read.
5. Failure to avoid physical distraction. When using the channel of meetings, for example, distractions including people moving in and out, heat, lighting, crowded condition, etc., often obstruct successful sending of message.
6. Failure of an audience to listen or look carefully. The only messages that get through to an audience are those which are heard, seen or experienced. An unfortunate tendency of people is not to give undivided attention to the communicator.
7. Failure to use enough channels parallel and also the use of too many channels in a series.

***Treatment of message***

Treatment has to do with the way a message is handled to get the information across to an audience. It deals with the design of methods for presenting the messages. Designing treatment usually requires original thinking, deep insight into the principles of human behaviour and skill in using refined techniques of message presentation. Great teachers are adequate in all ways, but are superb in their ability to treat messages.

The following are the three categories of bases useful for varying treatment:

## A. Matters of General Organization

1. Repetition or frequency of mention of ideas and concepts.
2. Contrast of ideas.
3. Chronological—compared to logical, compared to psychological.
4. Presenting one side compared to two-sides of an issue.
5. Emotional compared to logical appeals.
6. Starting with strong arguments compared to saving them until the end of presentation.
7. Inductive compared to deductive.
8. Proceeding from general to specific.
9. Explicit drawing conclusions compared to learning conclusions implicit for the audience to draw.

### *B. Matters of speaking and acting*

1. Limit the scope of presentation. Too many ideas at one time are confusing.
2. Be yourself strive to be clear.
3. Know the facts, fuzziness means sure death to a message.
4. Do not read your speech. People have more respect for a communicator who is sure of his subject.
5. Know the audience, each audience has its own personality. Be responsive to it.
6. Avoid being condescending. Do not talk or act down to people, or over their heads, never over-estimate the knowledge of an audience or underestimate his intelligence.
7. Effective treatment requires sincerity, smoothness, enthusiasm, warmth, flexibility and appropriateness of voice, gestures, movements and tempo.
8. Use alternative communicators when appropriate, as in group discussions, interviews, etc.
9. Remember that audience appeal is a psychological bridge to getting a message delivered.
10. Quit on time and gain audience goodwill.

***C. Matters of Symbol Variation and Device for Representing Ideas.***

1. Word symbols—speech
2. Real objects
3. Models
4. Specimens
5. Photographs
6. Graphs
7. Charts
8. Motion pictures
9. Slides
10. Drama
11. Puppets
12. Songs
13. Flash cards, etc.

Treatment of message is a creative task that has to be tailor-made for each instance of communication.

***The Audience***

Obviously, an audience is the intended receiver of messages. The 'pay off' in communication is dependent on what the audience does in response to messages. The following points help a communicator to clarify the exact nature of an audience and how to reach it:

1. Communication channels established by the social organization.
2. The system of values held by the audience—what they think is important.
3. Forces influencing group confirmity—custom, tradition, etc.
4. Individual personality factors—susceptibility to change, etc.
5. Native and acquired abilities—educational, economic and social levels.
6. Pressure of occupational responsibility—how busy or concerned they are.
7. People's needs as they see them, and as the professional communicators see them.
8. Why the audience is in need of changed ways of thinking, feeling and doing.
9. How the audience view the situation.

It is useful to communicators to understand these and other traits of an audience in making their plan for communication.

### *Communication and the Extension Worker*

It is much essential for an extension worker to learn the principles of effective communication and become a good communicator because the extension workers have to do the following :

1. Acquaint themselves with all the families in the village and learn their problems, needs and capabilities.
2. Survey the entire village, its people and their resources.
3. Learn from people and help people, help themselves work with people of all castes and creed and show them how to do things through actual participation.
4. Make serious planning and preparation for the demonstration classes; help the villagers work co-operatively, encourage to have discussions and develop leadership qualities in them. He has to help them not only to gain confidence but also income and encourage them to become active member of our republic in its social, economic and political life.

The communication process is now enveloped in a complex of highly developed techniques which have been applied with varying success to a wide range of situations. Communication is a process of sharing of experiences till they become a common possession. It is an act by which a person shares the knowledge, feelings, ideas, information, etc. for a common understanding. The extension worker (communicator) to communicate effectively, must understand the factors affecting his communication behaviour, the people with whom he works, those people's problems, the procedures for securing help, the methods of utilising the help of practical application to the problems, and the evaluation by each individual of his success in solving his problem.

# 8

# MEDIA FOR EXTENSION

The statement, "one good visual which can secure and maintain attention and educate the views in the desired area, is worth a thousand words" is quite correct. It is usually stated as "we learn 1 per cent through taste, 1,5 per cent through touch, 3.6 per cent through smell, 11 per cent throsugh learning, 83 per cent through sight. Similarly, we remember 10 per cent of what we read, 20 per cent of what we hear, 30 per cent of what we see, 50 per cent of what we see and hear, 80 per cent of what we say and 90 per cent of what we say as we do a thing. "If I hear I forget if I see I remember, if I do I know is verb".

Over the years mankind has successfully developed new technologies, of needed improvement in the quality of learning, experiences of the individual.

## Meaning of Audio-visual Education

There should be an understanding of the expression "audio-visual". This term has been given greater importance in recent years because of the fact that these aids are found to be effective in the classroom in motivating the students through two senses—hearing and sight. As W.M. Erikson rightly says, "The Audio-visual technology makes use of varied educational media to improve the efficiency of the teaching-learning situations".

## Visual Aids in Ancient Indian Education

Although audio-visual education in the modern sense of the expression is a movement of recent growth, visual aids, though not the modern scientific aids, wherein the old days in India.

Primitive men conveyed their ideas through drawings and developed and vocabulary to express them orally.

The tradition of drawing pictures on palm leaves which can be traced to the tenth century AD continued for a long time in India. The beautiful carvings which we find in ancient buildings and temples throughout the country also show clearly the importance which Indian educators attached to visual aids in those days. Patas pictures painted on cloth and picture sets were used and oral explanation was given. The painters of old days used cotton cloth for their scrolls though from the 15th century onwards hand made papers was generally used. Puppetry was also a popular art in villages in ancient India. Another variety of audio-visual education in ancient India was shadow-play with thin cut-out puppets made from a finepiece of cow or buffalo hide rendered translucent through scropping.

## Audio-Visual Aids in Modern Indian Education

A key to excellence in teaching is an acceptance and understanding of all children and their individual differences. The essence of best teaching is that the subject matter has to be communicated effectively to the students to make them understand the basic ideas. Effective communication can no longer be possible with words alone. Our traditional 'chalk and talk' method finds it difficult to motivate learners. The teacher often understands the difficulty of conveying ideas and information without using resources beyond words.

The foundation of all learning consists in representing clearly to the senses sensible objects so that they can be appreciated easily. An outstanding development in modern education should be increased use of supplementary devices by which the teacher through the use of more than one sensory channel helps to clarify, establish and correlate accuracy of concepts, interpretations and appreciation; increase knowledge rouse interest and even evoke worthy emotions and enrich the imagination of children.

Over the years mankind has successfully developed new technologies, as older methods have proved to be insufficient in the face of needed improvement in the quality of learning experiences of the individual. Knowledge in diverse fields is fast expanding today. To enable our learners to keep pace with this widening frontiers of knowledge our teaching has to be geared up.

***Why to Use Audio Visual Aids?***

They stimulate interest in learning, help to economise time and effort, best attention compellers, reduce verbalism in teaching procedure, provide rich aesthetic experience to the learners, break monotony and give variety to the classroom instruction.

These aids provide experiences not easily secured by other means and contribute in the efficiency, depth and variety of learning. Research findings exhibit the following values of audio-visual aids:

Contribution to factual learning, understanding is enhanced, learning is made permanent, influences attitudes, hightens at motivational and interest level, develop habits and skills and encourages voluntary reading.

## Classification of Audio-Visual Aids

Edgar Dale, the chief exponent of audio-visual aids to teaching speaks of the 'Cone of Experience'. Fig. 8.1 shows "audio-visual methods in teaching" (Holt, 1964).

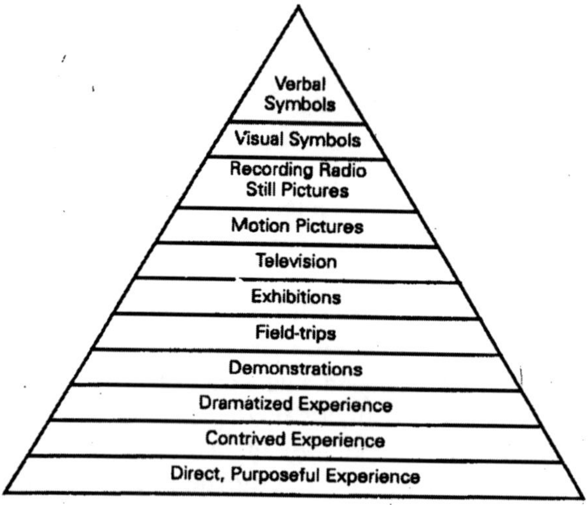


**Fig. 8.1: Cone of Experience of Edge Dale.**

***Direct, Purposeful Experience***

It is the direct reality as we experience it first hand. It is the purposeful experience of seeing, handling, tasting, touching, feeling and smelling. It is learning by doing and experiencing.

***Contrived Experience***

It is a simplified working model either by enlarging or containing that makes the real life experience easier to understand. It is also called as 'editing' of reality.

***Dramatised Experience***

This helps us to get closer to certain realities that are not available at first hand. Schools often dramatise a Parliament in session, in the classroom.

***Demonstration***

This is a visual explanation of an important fact, idea of process. For example, demonstration of experiments done in the farm, classroom or at home.

***Field Trips***

Through excursion, journeys and field trips we see, hear, touch and taste the objects in their natural selling which provide first hand knowledge.

***Exhibits***

Exhibits consist of charts, posters, working models, photographs, etc. arranged in a meaningful way. This may be a specific theme.

***Television***

Television brings use the real image as it happens, both video and audio. We could see and listen.

***Motion Pictures***

These, unlike filmstrips, may compress time and space. In a filmstrip to a steel mill, for example, we may follow each of the process from beginning to end. But a film on steel making can quickly pass over the less important process and emphasize the more significant ones.

### *Recording, Radio Still Pictures*

These materials have been roughly classified as 'one sense as these materials appeal to only one sensory organ, either ears or eyes are involved in learning.

### *Visual Symbols*

Here there is no longer a realistic reproduction of an object or event, but an abstract reproduction. We must see that the symbolic aids are geared to the level of the learners.

### *Verbal Symbols*

These are the designations which bear no physical resemblances of the original. The word 'horse' does not look like a horse, sound like a horse or feel like a horse.

The selection of aids depends on the nature of the subject taught and on the maturity of the learners.

### *Different Kinds of Teaching Aids*

The different kinds of teaching aids are listed below :

*Display Boards*

Black-board/chalk-board, Bulletin-board, Flannel-board/Felt-board, Hook and loop-boards, Magnetic boards, Plasticgraph boards, Peg boards.

*Graphic Aids*

Photographs, pictures, Posters, Charts and Graphs, Diagrams, Cartoons, Flash cards, Wet mounting, Maps, Comics, Illustrations (flat pictures).

*Three Dimensional Materials*

Models (dimunitives and enlargements), Specimen (replica) Objects, Mock-ups, Dioramas.

*Audio-aids*

Radio, Record player/disc recording, Tape-recorder, Gramophone, Public address equipment.

*Projected Aids*

Slide projector, Filmstrip projector, Films, Overhead projector, Epidiascope, Television, Video.

*Activity Aids* .

Excursion, contrived experience, experiments, etc.

## Hints for Effective Usage of Some Audio-Visual Aids

### *Black board/chalk board*

Chalk board is the basic, more versatile tool used for instruction. It is one of the simplest and oldest of visual aids. Chalk boards can be of different colours.

### *Use of Colour Chalk*

On different coloured chalk boards specific colour chalks could be used for maximum contrast. The learner finds it easy to look at the board when contrast coloured chalks are used, as it is listed in Table 8.10.

**Table 8.1. Types of Boards and Chalks**

| | *Boards* | *Chalks* |
|---|---|---|
| 1. | Green chalk-board | - White (or) yellow chalk |
| 2. | Grey | - Yellow |
| 3. | Red | - Green, Yellow |
| 4. | Orange | - Blue, or light green |
| 5. | Yellow | - Blue |
| 6. | Pink | - Purple, dark, blue |
| 7. | Black | - Any colour. |

On glass and plastic boards, felt pens could be used instead of chalk but special cleaning fluid should be used for wiping. Writings on chalk board should be erased using a dry duster made of any type of cloth or felt.

### *Some hints for using the chalk-board*

The following rules for using the chalk-board would definitely increase its effectiveness as a visual aid:

1. Do not fill the chalk-board with too many concepts.
2. Make the material simple, precise and brief statements are more effective than long sentences.
3. Plan your work on the chalk board in advance.
4. Gather everything you need for the chalk-board before the group meets.
5. Check lighting conditions. Chalk-board glare should be avoided.
6. The writing on the board should be visible at a distance, clear and legible.

7. Erase all unwanted material which distracts attention.
8. While writing, you should talk or narrate what is being done.
9. Prepare complicated chalk-board layouts before the group meets.

***Bulletin Board items***

Bulletin boards may be used to display numerous items such as personal announcements, booklets and brouchers, bulletins, cartoons, charts, diagrams, posters, maps, newspaper clippings, drawings, graphs, notices, pictures, pamphlets, photographs, postcards, models and specimens, subject outlines, trainee progress records (Table 8.2).

**Table 8.2. Effective Bulletin Board-planning and Arranging Displays**

| | | |
|---|---|---|
| 1. Select a specific topic | : | Use one central theme. Start the bulletin board with an idea and not a picture. |
| 2. Select the right materials | : | Preparation of bulletin boards is greatly fecilitated if a file of display materials is organised and maintained for ready use in the classroom. |
| 3. Plan the arrangement | : | (a) Thumb nail sketches are always a help in planning a proposed bulletin board.<br>(b) Arrange the materials in a pleasing and interesting way. |
| 4. Use Colour | : | (a) Colourful backgrounds, mounting and accessories catch the eye.<br>(b) Use colour harmony and balance. |
| 5. Use clear and neat writing | : | Through well-planned arrangement and well-planned labels. |
| 6. Make the arrangement tell | : | Through well-planned arrangement and well-planned labels. |
| 7. Add eyecatchers to the display | : | A spot colour, arresting captions and an interesting design. |
| 8. Avoid overcrowding exhibits | : | Space the material on the board. |
| 9. Use originality | : | More interesting and challenging to the students. |

### *Flannel Boards*

Flannel boards are not expensive and they can also be made. It is also called as Felt Board or Khadi Board. These boards are meant for use in classrooms and have to be of three or four feet high. Mas and stories can be built up in a dramatic way using flannel boards.

### *Hook and Loop Boards*

These boards are intended to support heavy three dimensional objects and flat material. These boards can also be used as felt boards.

### *Magnetic Boards*

Steel backed chalk boards provide added utility of a surface that can be used either for a chalk-board or for a magnetic board or for both in combination.

## Graphic Aids

Graphic aids are the form of visuals that are represented on plain surface. Graphics are only two dimensional. Examples of graphic aids are as follow:

*Photographs*

Photographs of field trips, group work drama etc. being interest among the pupils and they remember the recreational and social activities.

*Pictures*

These are useful to show comparisons; pictures should have artistic in quality, clarity, truthfulness, interest and suitability.

*Posters*

It is a medium to draw attention to an important aspect at a glance, e.g. family planning poster.

"We Two Ours One"

### *How to make effective posters?*

The following are some useful steps to prepare effective posters.

*(a) Illustration on picture.* It should be such as to bring out the message clearly at a glance. If it is a drawing, the actual thing to

be shown should be broughtout in bold relief. Avoid unnecessary details so that the viewer's attention is not confused. If you use a photograph, avoid unwanted surroundings and bring out the point prominently. While preparing illustrations keeps in mind the experience of the audience and use objects familiar to them.

*(b) Caption in Words.* Caption should be as small as possible. A five words caption is the best. Never write the caption vertically as it creates difficulty in reading. Do not break the caption.

*(c) Colour.* Use bright attractive colours. The centre core can be highlighted with a more prominent colour. Even in the caption some prominent word can be given a different colour. Do not use more than three colours, it may be confusing. Do not use odd combination of colours.

*(d) Space.* If poster is loaded with pictures and words the viewer gets lost so provide adequate space.

*(e) Layout.* It should be well-balanced so that the viewer's eyes can travel smoothly and quickly through the caption and illustration. It should hold the attention and clearly bring out the message to the viewer.

*(f) Check.* After the rough layout is complete show it to some people of the level of your audience. If there is any misconception or ambiguity remove it.

The poster should recommend action. It should be placed where people pass or gather. It should give only one idea and details should be given through other media.

## Charts and Graphs

A chart can present any information other than geographical in an easy-to-understand way. It is defined as "a visual symbol summarizing or comparing or contrasting or performing other helpful services in explaining subject matter".

### *How to Prepare Charts?*

Like posters, little skill is necessary to make charts. In making charts the following points however, should be remembered:

(i) Charts like any other pictorial material should be sufficiently large to be seen easily. The producer of charts should be clear about the conditions under which they will be seen.

(ii) Charts can tell a story in some detail but it should not contact too many words.

(iii) They should be strong enough to stand rough use.

(iv) They should be attractive to look at.

(v) As the main point about a chart is that it should be clearly understood by all those who are intended to study it, it should not contain any picture which is not related at all to their experience.

## Three Dimensional Materials

### *Models*

Models simplify reality. As they are three dimensional, they evoke greater interest and gives clear concept. Model concreatise abstract concepts. They simplify complex concepts. It could be used for regular classroom teaching because of its compact dimension. A large process could be easily demonstrated by a model as they provide interior views of objects and machines. A working model will secure immediate attention and will serve as a motivator. Models should be used only if it is not possible to get real objects where and other aids would not be helpful to give a better explanation.

### *Specimens*

Specimens are representations of complete objects whereas models are exact replicas of real objects. Specimens are unitary in nature. Students, profit by understanding and observing the real nature of an object.

### *Objects*

An object is a real thing. Any concrete objects shown to pupils will enable them to have a correct concept of the object. Objects of similar class but of different varieties can be presented before the students.

### *Mock-ups*

When the direct first hand experience is either impractical or impossible, mock-ups can be used. A mock-up may be defined as an operating models, usually at full scale, designed to be worked with directly by the learner for specific training or analysis. Mock-up is an imitation of a real thing, some elements of the real thing may be purposely eliminated in order to focus attention on others. Mock-ups are very useful in giving training in complex skills.

### *Dioramas*

A diorama is a three dimensional scene in depth incorporating a group of modelled objects and figures in a natural setting. The diorama scene is set-up on a small stage with a group of modelled objects kept on the foreground which is blended into a painted realistic background. The objects in a diorama are not made to scale. For representation of depth, objects kept at the background are made considerable smaller, to create an illusion. When colour is used in appropriate ways, diorama had vividness and realism.

### *Audio Aids*

Audio aids such as radio, taperecorder mostly appeal to the ears of the learners. A tape recorder can be used for many purposes. The uses mostly depend upon the imagination of the teacher and the taught.

It helps the extension worker and the learner alike to hear the recording of their voices and makes them much more critical of their own speech, thereby it provides an effective means of self-instruction. It enables the extension worker to be in more than one place at a time. It facilitates editing of sounds shortening, eliminating or adding of materials from different sources. It helps in preservation of sounds for future use. It can be used for evaluation of sounds. It helps transportation of sounds from one place to another. It is used for duplication of sounds. It helps in synchronisation of sound with pictures. It is used in the learning and teaching of music. It helps in practice of public speaking, and it is used for rectifying defective speech.

### *Gramophone Records*

Talks and songs can be preserved in disc and played when desired. The disc can be played repeatedly and stopped at any point of discussion, or programme.

### *Public Address Equipment*

A public address system include microphone, amplifier and loudspeaker. The microphone converts soundwaves into alternating electric currents which are fed into the amplifier. The amplifier is an electronic device to amplify these electric currents. The amplified electric current fluctuates in accordance with the vibrations of the soundwaves. When these amplified electric currents are fed into the loudspeaker, it converts them into soundwaves and we hear the loud voice of the speaker. All these process take no time to be completed and so the sound picked up by the microphone is reproduced simultaneously by the loud-speaker.

Microphone → Amplifier → Loudspeaker.

### *Projected Aids*

When a projected aid is used, an enlarged image of the material is projected on a screen kept at a distance from the projector. The room is either, totally or to be more effective than a non-projected aid since a darkened room reduced distraction and the bright image on the screen secures the attention of the audience easily. Colour will make the aid more attractive; will make the aid more dynamic and motion associated with sound will be more effective and attention compelling than the non-projected aids.

## Slides

The lantern slide is one of the oldest form of projected pictures.

### *Effective ways of using slides*

To use the slides effectively first determine the right spot for slides in the lesson plan, secure slide catalogues, choose the correct slides, make your own slides for specific lessons, arrange slides showing order with the thumb mark in the upper right hand corner, keep the projector ready and set up screen before the arrival of the audience have extra projector lamp, plugs and extension card available, check seating arrangement ventilation, arrange an adequate signal if using a projector operator, prepare and motive learner before presenting slides, present slides in a psychological and orderly fashion, leave image on screen long enough to permit learner read, use a pointer to focus attention on specific points in the picture, use slides in connection with other audio-visual aids, apply slide information as soon as possible, test learners understanding, and reshow slides if necessary.

## Filmstrips

### *Characteristics of Filmstrip*

Filmstrips are composed of a series of still pictures and titles of captions placed in sequential order on 35 mm film from 2 to 6 feet long, with sprocket holes on each side. They are commonly between twenty and fifty frames (individual pictures) in length. Filmstrips are produced in black and white or colour.

Some of the more common purposes for using filmstrips are to provide a basis for understanding symbols and to help teach skills.

Because filmstrips can be projected at any speed and be repeated in whole or in part, they are suitable for group instruction in learning skills, such as making silk-screen frames and using card catalogues.

It provides information probably the majority of uses of filmstrips fall into this category ... presenting factual data in visualized form.

Another use of filmstrip is to stimulate aesthetic appreciations many filmstrips, particularly those in colour may be used to build aesthetic appreciation of beatury, rhythm, and form in nature or in great works of art.

To develop interest in further pursuit of topics filmstrips are often used during introductory stages of unit teaching to present striking information or to set up important problems. Through such showings, students are encouraged to carry on further activities library research, writing, report making, drawing or painting.

The film strip could also be used to consolidate and "review" learnings toward the end of a unit, a filmstrip may be used to help students look back over what they have studied and to view it in the light of important learnings.

It is often advantageous to capitalise upon the ability of the filmstrip to focus group attention upon a lighted screen in a darkened room.

To supplement and reinforce learnings from other experiences we could use filmstrip. Students who have taken a field trip to study in their local community may be helped by viewing and discussing a filmstrip on the same subject.

Filmstrip can provide opportunities for students to practice basic skills. Students may be given the responsibility for selecting and showing filmstrips to others in the class. The filmstrip provides unusual opportunities to help students learn to verbalise about what they see—an activity aimed at clarifying and strengthening learnings.

## Overhead Projectors

One of the newest type of projectors to join the audio-visual family is the overhead projector. This machine projects the image from a transparency back over the operators shoulder to a screen. Light is furnished by a 500 to 1000 watt lamp and is reflected upward to a projection stage.

### *Transparencies*

Transparencies are large slides for use with an overhead projector from the front of a room. Transparencies can visually present concepts, processes, facts outlines and summarises to small groups to average-size classrooms and to large groups.

Because of its many applications the overhead projector has become accepted widely as a basic teaching tool. The ease with which instructors can make and use transparencies and the effectiveness of their use in learning has caused many institutions to equip classroom and lecture halls with overhead projectors.

### *Advantages of Using Overhead Projectors*

The important and specific advantages of transparencies had made it a special projected visual aid.

1. The overhead projector is used in front of the class by the instructor who has complete control of the sequence, timing and manipulating of his material.

2. Facing the class and observing student reactions, the instructor can guide the audience, control their attention and regulate the flow of information in the presentation.

3. The projected image behind the instructor can be made as large as necessary for all audience to see. The brilliantly illuminated image is visible even in an undarkened room.

4. The large transparency projector itself is simple to operate and requires only minimal servicing. It may be placed on a low stand beside which the operator is seated or it may be used on a disc or table or built in as permanent classroom fixture.

5. Materials for instructional presentation can be of many types, i.e., photographic, written or drawn, graphic, pictorial, verbal or combinations of these. They may be prepared in various colours or in black and white or again in combination of these. A technique called 'technamation' (a process of utilising polarisation of light) will even permit the simulation of motion in still pictures.

6. Since the transparency as it is placed on the projector is seen by the instructor exactly as students see it on screen he may point, write or otherwise make indications upon it to facilitate communication.

### *Direct Experiences*

Learning experiences which are real, life like and available to the learner for first-hand souiting, questioning and recognition are likely to be the most effective avenues through which children become informed about the social and natural environment.

### *Museums and Exhibits*

Through museums and exhibits concrete examples of materials and objects are present to the child. The teacher has to plan for the exhibition in accordance to the educational needs of the child which helps the child get much of the information included in various lessons. According to the Secondary Education Commission, museums serve to educate the public at large and give them a realistic approach to scientific investigations and scientific discoveries.

### *Demonstrations*

Demonstration is a technique which is often used by all teachers teaching various subjects. Ideas, skills, attitudes and process can be demonstrated. The spoken word is supplemented with demonstration using varied aids resulting in auditary and visual learning.

## Mass Media in Education

For a long period, and till today the audio-visual aids have been assisting the extension worker in his/her work. However, the effectiveness of those aids depend on how effective the person is in handling those aids. Over the years, the audio-visual aids have been changed with the change in technology. Later on, with the advent of electronic revolution the education system started making use of the mass media to impart more knowledge to the learners.

### *Various Mass Media*

There are many mass media in vogue in India. They are:

(1) Radio, (2) TV, (3) CCTV, (4) Video Cassettes, (5) S.I.T.E Programmes, (6) INSAT Programmes, (7) Multi-media Packages.

### *Radio*

Though television has been found to possess many positive attributes as a powerful communication media, it has been widely recognised today that due to the limitations of channels and therefore, of languages broadcast, neither the satellite system nor the torestrial system can cover the entire country. The results of the efforts made to use the simpler and more economical technology to meet India's economic, social, linguistic and geographical requirements is the effective utilisation of radio for broadcasting extension educational programmes throughout the country.

### *Types of Radio Lesson*

Radio lesson are generally of two types, enrichment and direct teaching. Under the first category we can include those broadcasts which do not bear directly on specific topics but provide ample background information to these topics. For example, trip to Kashmir'–A talk by some experts. This cannot be considered as a geography lesson, but it can prove to be a useful information giving lesson.

These programmes of direct teaching are extremely helpful because they are prepared by specialists devoting considerable time on study and preparation.

### *Nature of the Medium*

Radio as mass communication tool can inform, stimulate the curiosity, arouse and build interest, create the desire to learn, see, hear and act, widen horizons and mental outlook, break down prejudices and bring enlightment, promote favourable attitudes and influence emotions, inspire to some form of action, interpret policies, guide listeners interest and help them grasp the significance of new ideas and thoughts.

### *Television*

Television means seeing at a distance. Television is a combination of seeing and hearing, similar to motion pictures. Television in considered to be a "window of the word" or a "magic box" as it brings stimulating materials is from the world at large into the classroom. There are three types of television programme. They are commercial, educational and instructional.

*Commercial Television.* Commercial Television Programmes are meant for the general public, entertainment, information advertisment and news are main broadcasts.

*Educational Television.* ETV programme are designed to affect viewers behaviours, knowledge, attitudes and values in specific areas. For example, agricultural programmes meant for the farmers, house keeping for home makers, etc.

*Instructional Television.* ITV programme is frequently associated with the regular school and college or university programme. It is designed to influence the knowledge, skills and aptitudes of students. It is organised much like a class in a college or school. It consists of sequence of connected session. The school children (or) college students attend each session and carry out some assignment e.g. UGL Countrywide classroom.

### *Advantages of Television*

Television makes use of sight, sound and motion. Teaching by television has the following unique advantages:

It is a convenient and economical means of reaching enormous cross–section of the population with simultaneous presentation. It combines the best elements of radio (going right into the home or classroom) with the potency of motion pictures. Television is capable of helping to overcome learning barriers for many persons—presenting important ideas, helping to mould attitudes, providing information in ways, which demand neither high verbal proficiency nor physical presence at the scene of action. It is a means of multiplying the "personal" contacts for outstanding television instructors with students and adults all over the country or the world. It is capable of helping to bring about needed social change and development. It capitalises upon immediacy, upon the "here and now" aspects of communication. It presents the natural phenomena of the world in actual form. For example, landing on moon and exploration provide vivid concept with reality. Microscopic forms of life can be magnified, photographed and presented on television and made visible from the naked eye. Slow growth process can be accelerated. For example, the stages in the development of a child which actually extends over several hours or days may be presented in few seconds. Television portrays past events. The past events can be brought to life through dramatizations on television, and television presentations are universal that any viewer, regardless of sex, race or economic status can benefit out of them.

### *Video*

The introduction of colour TV has been closely followed by another impact in our culture, i.e. video films. The video films have invaded and spread in the cities like wild fire. No doubt, video is a luxury in a poor country like India. But, now we are in a position to accept it and make the most out of it. We have to think ahead and plan for its maximum utilization in a variety of ways.

### *Use of Television–Video in the Classroom*

1. It is obvious that visual stimulus induces interest. The added interest increases learner motivation and this is an important consideration.

2. Good reason for using a video is the opportunity it provides for learners to hear authentic language used in context. This is very important for students residing in remote towns and villages where there is no opportunity for listening to a foreign language.

The most significant use, is to provide practice in listening comprehension. Further video-TV are useful as, stimulating sources of information, stimuli for discussion, instruments for provocation, illustrations of specific language items pure entertainments, and it is useful in giving professional training, it provides supplementary or remedial programmes for the children with specific learning difficulties.

Video can be used to exhibit a film, record an official programme from the domestic TV channel and play it for the class, record our own programme and play it to the class, record a lecture given by an expert to an audience and play it to the class, cut the sound off and show short silent sequences, buy already recorded video-cassettes available in the market on different themes and play them.

### *How to make Video Lessons More Effective?*

Four simple strategies are employed in any Video-Class. Silent Viewing, prediction, description, and assignment.

*Silent Viewing.* Showing learners a scene with the sound turn off and asking them to interpret what they have seen.

*Prediction.* Stopping the video or freezing a frame and asking the viewers to interpret what will happen next.

*Description.* Asking learners to describe what they have been watching, over a period.

*Assignment.* Providing the learners with some written assignments on video contents.

### *Indian National Satellite (INSAT-IB)*

The First INSAT (IB) was launched on August 30, 1983 and is fully operational from October 25, 1983. Afterwards many more satellites were launched.

The role of INSAT in education has consumed greater importance. It moves away from curriculum oriented approach, emphasis is on direct teaching and aims at improving quality of education. It stimulates public interest on news and current affairs, games and sports and other important events.

The television programmes were telecasted by utilising the facilities provided by SITE (Satellite Instructional Television Experiment). These programmes were designed to demonstrate the new approach to school science teaching. It also provides opportunities for upgrading the teacher's knowledge and understanding of the subject matter.

### *Closed Circuit Television (CCTV)*

Close circuit TV is a transmission system that distributes television programmes live on tape, both audio and video, to a limited network connected by a cable. The network may consist of one school, a whole school district or several districts. The telecast cannot be received by other Television sets outside the network. CCTV is more effective in Teacher Education. Teacher Trainees can have immediate feedback when they do microteaching.

## Computer in Education

Science and technology are playing a significant role in the formation of modern civilization and aculturation of the society. Day by day there is increase in scientific and technogical impact, upon human-life activities in developing the scientific attitude of individual in society. Mechanisation is dominating in today's life. In this continuum, a new field has emerged in education technology and that is computer based education.

The common acronyms in computer based education (CBE) are as follows :

CAL - Computer Assisted/Aided Learning

CML - Computer Managed Learning

CBT - Computer Based Training

CAI - Computer Assisted/Aided Instruction.

### *Computer-aided Instruction*

It is a general term referring to the fact that the computer aids the traditional instruction process in some manner. The main strength of the computer as a learning medium is its ability to process information very quickly and accurately.

### *Modes of CAL*

*Drill and Practice.* Perhaps the simplest form of CAL is the computer to present the learner with a series of exercises which he or she must complete by giving some response—an answer. The computer processes that response (according to the rules embodied in its programme) to determine whether or not it is "correct". Feedback and corrective messages are provided to the learner. Continuous drill and practice is provided, systematic mistakes and detached and the computer can adapt the pattern of exercises to rectify this weakness.

*Tutorial.* In its simplest form, tutorial dialogue bears a close resemblance to the programmed learning sequences found in the print and on teaching machines of the early 1960s. Since the computer can only follow pre-specified rules, it is difficult to arrange for it to exhibit very sophisticated intelligence and so present any real challenge to 'human tutor'. But, advance in artificial intelligence have led to programmes which can handle every complex structures of rules and influences, and can assist in the process of decision–making.

*Stimulations.* The 'drill and practice' and tutorial present information in a structured way. Another facet of learning involves the students real-life systems on phenomena. The computer can be used to emulate a real-life system by following a set of rules which approximates the behaviour of a real system. The advantage of stimulation is its flexibility and control which the computer can bring.

*Modelling.* The stimulation, is provided by the tutor. In modelling, the student has to construct the analogue. He has to "teach" the computer the rules, so that it can emulate the real-life system in given circumstances and correctly predict the behaviour of the real-life system in new circumstances. The student learns through this process and demonstrates his or her mastery of the learning through the final model.

*Interactive Knowledge Based System (IKBS).* The IKBS consists of a descriptive model of knowledge relating to a particular topic, system or situation. This can be explored by the learner, perhaps with an expert system providing tutorial guidance and explanation, or by means of asking questions which will lead to an understanding and assimilation of the knowledge.

*Browsing.* The power of the computer to store, retrieve and process information is used to help the student as he or she browses through the material, responding to questions about related information, retrieving items which are needed, summarising statistical data and suggesting possible lines of investigation that may be of interest.

### *Methods of using 'CAL' Materials in Teaching and Learning*

*Computer Assisted Teaching.* The CAL package can be used as a class demonstration, under the control of the teacher, either as the main focus of the lesson or to illustrate various points that may arise. This is similar to the laboratory demonstration or the use of a video tape with the whole class.

*Individual Learning.* This has often been criticized as an impersonal and determined method of learning. In part this is a reflection of the deterministic style of some tutorial material which resembles illuminated programmed instruction with the pages being turned by the computer.

*Small Group Learning.* The use of CAL with small groups offers many of the advantages of the classroom teaching and individualised methods while avoiding their disadvantages. A group of 2 or 3 students work with the CAL package discussing the course of their joint learning, their inputs to the package, and the resulting output. The dialogue among students is equally important as their dialogue with the computer serves to stimulate their discussions and confirm conclusions.

When a teacher gets trained in preparation of audio-visual aids and their effective use colleges or schools could jointly start resource centres of audio-visual aids and can be shared by other schools and colleges. This arrangement will promote the utilisation of educational technology to improve education.

Centre for Educational Technology (CET), a wing of NCERT is engaged in similar programme. The teachers are trained, post type teaching, learning materials are prepared and distributed to the educational institutions as part of their extension programme.

As the teacher's job in future is going to be more of guidance and supervisory due to advancement in science and technology they should be well equipped with the skill of preparation and use of soft-ware. They should be able to establish soft-ware and hard-ware Banks for distribution.

# 9

# LEADERSHIP IN EXTENSION

Leadership is a social phenomenon that exists everywhere throughout the world. It is a universal social institution that is seen in one form or another in every form of life. Every person who leads a group of people or a society is called a 'Leader'. People who influence in any shape of life are called leaders. Sprott, in his *Social Psychology* says. "Any one, who acts as model to others is often called a leader". Leadership as defined by Lopiere, "is a behaviour that affects the behaviour of other people."

## The Extension Worker as an Effective Leader

In extension work, leaders are visualised as initiators of action which helps a group move in the direction, it wishes to move. The pattern of leadership in Indian villages is still primarily based on heredity and caste structure, village landlords or zamindars, the village heredity type of leaders. Besides these, there are two other forms of leaderships which exist in villages today. The first one is personal leadership. In several villages there are persons who are looked upon and respected because of their knowledge or wide experience. This type of leadership truly leads people. After Independence, with the establishment of village panchayats and growth of the co-operative movement and the rural extension programme, another type of leadership has evolved in rural India which appears to be replacing the traditional types of leadership.

Extension work needs local leaders who can guide the community according to its cherished ideals and towards its goals. These leaders are those who emerge through the democratic process, work in accordance with the democratic principles and ideals and have the general welfare of the community, at their heart.

The extension worker, as a effective leader, should be able to identify the potential rural leaders. He should be able to know and use some of the techniques which are useful in this process. If he does not identify these leaders, he will not be able to develop and use the leadership that is available in the village community. He is a hired worker who has no official authority over the people with whom he works. He needs, therefore the ability to find leaders among the local people who will volunteer to work with him.

## Identifying Local Leadership

Leadership arises out of needs and needs can be created for the leadership to grow and finally get trained for proper action. Leadership is always present in any situation; what is required is a faith or belief, on the part of the extension worker, in the potential leadership of local men and women.

In all group situations, we can find an element of leadership. A careful and constant observation will help the extension worker in spotting leaders. Through experience the extension worker can identify the potential and resourceful leaders in the community. Leadership is specific and in identifying leaders, it is important to know the following facts :

1. The job to be performed.
2. What characteristics and skills this job requires.
3. Whether the person possesses the needed qualification.
4. What group will support or follow this person?
5. Of the qualities he has:
   (a) Which of them may be improved by training.
   (b) Which may not be changed.
6. Of the qualities he lacks:
   (a) Which may be developed.
   (b) Which may not be developed.
7. The basis on which he can be induced to work.

In selecting or identifying leaders, it is important to know clearly what needs to be done and what knowledge and skills are needed to do it. Some complications may arise due to the condition such as health, energy and intelligence subject-matter knowledge ability to plan talk and ability to organise. When the extension worker knows what qualifications are needed, it is easier to find a leader. In doing so, it is important to find a person that the group will support or follow:

Though locating local leaders is a difficult task, the following methods are proved to be workable in this respect.

The extension worker should constantly observe a community of group in action. This will enable him to spot potential leaders. He may observe the community in any type of situation. For obtaining the best results, the groups should not be aware of his observation.

### *Discussion Method*

Through discussions (on any subject) the person with sound knowledge and ability can be recognised and a mere talker easily spotted.

### *Workshop Method*

Through workshop method, we can identify the leader. The large group breaks up into smaller groups and the responsibility of the programme and decision-making rests upon the smaller units and the leadership emerages from each group.

### *Questionnaire or Sociometric Method*

Sociometric method is employed by the professional worker or extension worker who goes into a new community and wants to find out which people are the potential leaders, or what is the leadership status.

### *Election Method*

Ancther method of identifying a local leader is that of election in helping groups elect the right people for the right jobs, state clearly to the group the positions required as well as the kinds of jobs each person is expected to perform. With an understanding of the kinds of work each leader or officer is to do the group can vote more wisely.

## Personality Dynamics of a Leader

Like other individual human beings leader carries with him his past experience, emotional tendencies, goals and needs as well as personal standards. Followers generally rate their leaders on the higher scoring of various personality dynamic factors. In addition to these due to environmental and socio-psycho-interactional process, a leader acquires a better self-concept of himself (Fig. 9.1).

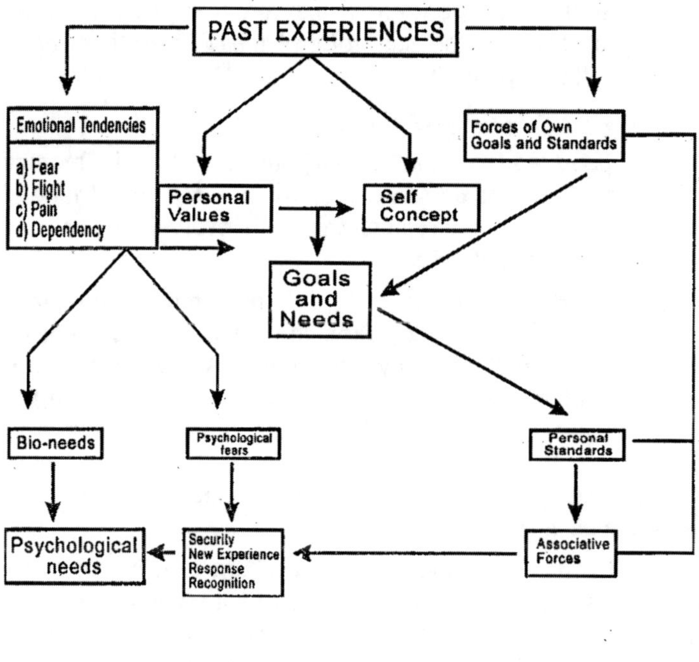


**Fig. 9.1. Personality Dynamics of a Leader.**

## Theories of Leadership

There are four theories that attempt to explain the phenomenon of leadership.

**Trait Theory** — A person who possesses certain traits of excellence becomes the leader of the group.

**Functions** — It is not the mere possession of some superior generalised traits that enable a person to become a leader for all types of responsibilities. It is the ability to perform the functions determines the potentiality of a person to be a leader. A good singer can be the leader of singing party and so would be a player.

**Situation** — Under certain circumstances, it is the situation that becomes more important in determining whether or not an individual will become a leader. When the situation changed from war to peace even Churchill, who was so successful during war, was exhifted from the position of leadership.

**Interaction** — It is now held that it is none of the aforesaid three theories independently explain the phenomenon of leadership fully. It is the sum total of these three theories that provide better explanation.

### *Characteristics of a good leader*

1. A good leader known herself/himself and all the members in the group and has genuine concern for every one. The leader should establish good relationship with every member of the team and emancipate them.

2. A good leader establishes fraternity among the members of the group. She/he recognises the rights of every one and ensures that all of them enjoy these rights. A good leader proves equal opportunity and transcends religious, linguistic, regional and sectional diversities to attain peace, unity and love among its members. He does not indulge in slander backbiting, jealousy and adverse criticism of others to build ones own reputation at the expense of another.

3. Sharing is another important characteristics of a good leader, sharing is the order of the day as it benefits each other. Sharing consists of an inter change of ones knowledge the warmth and the ideas. This builds cohesive feeling among the members of the group.

4. Service should be the motto of a good leader. A leader is being served by others and in turn the leader should serve others without any discrimination.

5. A good leader is a responsible person. He is ready to accept the difficulties and problems and takes the blame or credit for the success or failure of a task. Responsibility works

untiringly with selfless dedication to honour its commitments and responsibility begets greater responsibility.

6. A good leader is accountable to the group and the society. Responsibility and accountability are the two sides of the same coin. Responsibility means liability to be called to account, when incharge or control of an undertaking. Accountability assesses and measures the depth of man's responsibility and is related. It takes care of optimum use of time, money and every resources towards the best of results.

7. A leader should have a good manner. A responsible leader realises that he is there to serve not to boss and be autocratic. A good leader should be a master of good communication techniques and be able to share his views with others.

8. A good leader is also a good decision maker. Taking into consideration the pros and cons, advantages and disadvantages of the decision has to be taken. The decisions are based on the intelligence rather than individual.

9. Self-evaluation and one's consciousness guide a good leader.

### *Functions of a Leader*

The effective leader is said to be group oriented, fulfils group needs and oils the wheels of group interaction. A mouthpiece of his followers is only a hypocritical leadership style.

There are leaders who do not read the consensus, but impose it making objects of fear and reverence.

Followers can be bought, but the purchaser is not a leader; he is an employer. Domination can be achieved by force but sustained force is not a possibility. The right to dominate is voluntarily given to one who has the gift of leadership. Max Weber calls it as "charisma". Effective leaders command devotion. In some forms or other a leader should be a superhuman.

Every leader has to perform certain functions. These functions have been defined in different ways by different sociologists and social psychologists. Krech and Crutchrield have defined the functions of a leader in the following words:

"A leader must partake the same degree of function of executive, planner, policy maker, expert, extraordinary group representative, controller of internal relationship, purveyor of reward and punishment, arbitrator, a mediator and exampler"

Different aspects of the functions of a leader are being discussed below:

*Leader is an Executive*—As an excutive a leader has not only to guide and direct the behaviour of his followers but he has also to control their activities, so that they are able to discharge their obligation successfully.

*Leader is a Planner*—Every leader, in order to uphold the values and the objectives of the society has to draw certain plans. These plans reflect his imagination and capability. He has, therefore, to act as a planner, too.

*Leader is a Policy Maker*—Every society has to uphold certain objectives and values. These objectives and values can well be maintained when certain policies have been framed for maintaining them. These policies may either grow from below, or may be imposed from above or the leader may himself impose it. Even when the leader imposes his own policies, he has to take his followers into confidence.

*Leader is an Expert*—Every leader has to act as an expert. He has to know many things and know them thoroughly. Then only he can arouse confidence and respect from his followers.

*Leader is an External Group Representative*—This is not true about secondary groups than the primary social groups. In a primary social group, generally the head of the family is the leader but in a community or in any social group, some one has to act as its leader and spokesman. In that capacity the leader has to play an important role.

*Leader Controls Interrelationship*—The leader has to control, guide and direct the internal relationship of the group. Since he is well aware of the qualities and the advocates of the group, he can direct the internal relationship in a successful manner.

*Leader Rewards and Punishes*—Since the leader represents the will of the members of the group, he can grant recognition to certain persons and also penalise others. Those who act according to the wishes of the leader are rewarded, while those who are against the wishes are punished. These reward and punishment are acceptable and lasting when these are administered according to the will of the people and the values of the society.

*Leader is an Arbitrator and Mediator*—In social groups tensions occur occasionally. The leader has to act as arbitrator and meditor in order to keep the society and social relationship intact.

*Leader is a symbol of the Group*—The leader symbolises his group. He has, therefore, to maintain the unity within his group and also keep its various resources intact.

*Leader takes the Responsibility of Individual*—The leader assumes the responsibilities of the individual members of his group. Individual members of the group, are therefore, relieved of their responsibility as members of that group.

*Leader is an Ideologist*—The leader has to lay down the ideology of the group. It is this ideology that guides the actions of the group. This ideology may be political, social or spiritual.

*Leader plays Father Role*—A leader has to play the role of the father of the society as well. He has not only to protect the interest of his followers but also provide them with everything that would make their living successful.

*Leader is a Scapegoat*—A leader has also to become a scapegoat. When the society or the group that he leads does not succeed, all the blame is put on his shoulders. Followers start hating him and he is held responsible for everything that is bad or that went wrong.

***Base of power for Leadership***

French and Raven (1938) defined the following four bases of power:

*Reward Power*—These are based on the followers perception that the leader has the ability to mediate reward for them.

*Coertive Power*—These are based on the followers perception that there leader has the ability to mediate punishment for them.

*Legitimate Power*—These are based on the perception of the followers that their leader has a legitimate right to prescribe behaviour for them.

*Referent Power*—These powers based on the followers

identification with their leader and perception that the leader has some special knowledge or expertise.

### *Role and functions of local leaders*

The functions of local leaders in extension programmes vary from place to place and in accordance with the nature and scope of the job to be performed. In a country like India, where a majority of the population is not educated, the local leader has to function as a medium of education for others. The overall function of local leaders is to lead in different ways under a variety of situations. The functions of local leaders are varied, and depend upon specific group functions and the personal abilities they possess. Their role and functions are highly related to each other, and are sometimes mixed so much together that it becomes difficult to differentiate between the two. The major functions of local leaders are to set an example for others to follow.

Local leaders are those who show special interest and initiative in a local programme. They are the people who catch new ideas first. They serve the community without a profit motive. The satisfaction they get from their own action is their only reward and incentive. They do have other motives for taking initiative, but those are part of the psychological aspect of motivation.

Groups are dependent on leaders and without them they are helpless; leadership is associated with responsibility, what the leader does or fails to do directly affects the welfare of the group. The action of the group also affects the leader. The group usually helps him by according him respect and power. Mutual confidence permits the leader to have wide discretion and broad powers. What a local leader can easily do may require considerable time and effort for another.

One of the important roles which a local leader has to play in the community is that of the initiator, as has been pointed out earlier. If he waits for others to initiate action, then he is a leader in a nominal sense only. The amount of initiative or aggressiveness needed by the leader depends in part upon the group—one can exercise initiative without driving people. The person who studies his group will learn the amount of initiative required to get the group into action.

Groups usually need help of two kinds—help in making progress towards their working goals, and help in keeping the group in a healthy working condition. A good local leader is usually aware of both the needs and will play roles which will be in line with these two needs.

***Tasks expected from a leader***

Assistance to the group in identifying its needs, aid the group by setting some example before them, making the group move towards goals, encouraging and improving interaction among group members, keeping the group together, making resources available to the group demonstrating to make them believe, keeping themselves abreast with the latest technology and techniques, adopting themselves all the improved practices, organising meetings and other dicussions groups, serving as marketing advisers, supplying the improved equipment to the beneficiaries, assisting the beneficiaries to get assistance. Serving the people who want to follow innovative practices. Educating the clients to improve their practices, acting as liaison officers between the extension workers and the farmers. Educating the farmers in the latest agricultural technology. Helping the fellow-farmers in getting the needed agricultural inputs.

A leader sets an example for other members of his group and in this way he influences people to move towards the identified goal. Dwight Sanderson suggests five roles of a leader. They are as follows:

*Spokesman*—He or she has to speak for the people he or she is representing.

*Harmoniser*—He or she has to deal in a tactful way with persons who create conflicts in the group and bring them together in working towards group goals. He or she has to show his or her superiority by showing some useful ideas to the members of the group.

*Planner*—He or she to realise the needs of the group in advance and must have plans to fulfil them. He or she has to interpret the purposes of the group into practical goals and open the potentialities of available resources.

*Executives*—He or she helps the group in carrying out the plans and policies. He or she gets things done, stimulates others and promotes solidarity.

*Symbol*—He or she has to be loyal to the ideals of the group in words and action, must not be self-interested, represent the group.

Leaders and group-functioning are two sides of the same coin and linked with each other. In fact, there is a psychodynamics between the two. It is a kind of chicken-egg type or controversy to ask the questions whether it is an effective leader who enables a group to function effectively or is it the good group that gives birth to an effective leader. Both of these go hand-in-hand. There cannot be an effective leader unless there is a functional group, that he is leading, and surely a good functional group does provide fertile ground for leadership to appear and develop. The function of leadership is therefore to stimulate interaction, sentiment and action.

### *Training of Local Leaders*

The potential or local leaders who are identified with the help of the various methods may be recognised by others as having some leadership ability, and lack some. Here arises the problem of training local leaders so that they may be able to develop in themselves the essentials of good leadership. The objective of training of local leaders is to make them good teachers, capable of passing on many ideas and truths with a perfect understanding of the people with whom they are working. The training of local leaders brings about changes in their attitudes and alerts their knowledge, skills and sensitiveness towards themselves and others. This in turn leads to changes in the actual performance of the leaders in carrying out their roles.

The objective of leadership training vary with the type of job expected to be done. The training programme must be made specific in terms of particular group needs. However, the training must be such that it will also prepare persons for the generalised roles they will have to play.

The objectives of leadership training for a workshop as stated by Taba may apply to any kind of leadership training. These are as follows:

1. Mastering fundamental concepts that would serve as a framework for understanding and interpreting group behaviour, social learning, and cultural differences.
2. Methods of identifying and analysing problems, to promote the ability to see problems in perspective.
3. Develop competence in group processes; co-operative thinking, exchange and analysis of ideas, facts and teaching; processes of converting discussion into consensus; ability and disposition to conceive group goals; respect for and understanding of others.
4. Acquire technical skills necessary to carry out a job, diagnose situations, learn how to approach problems, plan appropriate educational procedures, learn skills in handing appropriate diagnostic techniques, conduct open discussion, learn team work with other leaders, etc.

### *Methods of Leadership Training*

It is difficult to separate methods which apply only to formal or informal leadership training. It should be kept in mind that the methods overlap in many situations. Formal methods of leadership training are those which are structured to achieve specific goals and are usually set up to train and develop leadership in others. Informal methods are not structured, but are those which the individual utilises in personal leadership.

#### *Informal*

One of the first requirements in training is that the leader learns to understand and deal with people. This is accomplished through personal observation and study of materials that relate to human behaviour. The following are the some methods of developing leadership by any individual.

*1. Observation*—By noticing how others have performed as effective leaders.

2. *Reading*—Studying printed material often found in the form of leader handbooks, newsletters, circulars, bulletins, etc.

*3. Talking*—Speaking with other leaders in the programme or related field of interest and also with members to determine consensus.

### *Formal*

The individual or local leader may take advantage of formal training programmes in the quest of becoming a better leader. Formal methods are either used individually or in combinations.

*Lecture*—This is probably the most common method. Through this method local leaders under training are given enough material for thought, but little opportunity for self-expression. The lecture method is effective in certain situations, but should usually be supplemented by other methods, depending on the objectives to be attained.

*Discussion and Workshop*—This is a method in which there will be active participation of the audience.

*Forum, Panel and Symposium*—In a forum or a panel, three to four individuals explain phases of a particular subject. In a symposium, two or more speakers with different points of view or areas of interest discuss the issue.

*Audio-Visuals Techniques*—Role-play, socio-drama and demonstration, are some of the audio-visual techniques.

*Field Trips*—Local leaders or potential leaders visit other groups and observe the action and behaviour of a successful organisations.

*Apprenticeship*—Here, the local leaders or the potential leaders see someone operating with a view to learning some of the activities and ways of handling; problems in the field of leadership. This serves as an instrument for the local leaders to acquire a better understanding of the job.

*Training Group*—This brings several local leaders to the training sessions at the same time. These people reinforce each other since each of them has experiences of his own.

*Direct Assistance from Experts*—This may come in the from of advice.

*Buzz Groups*—These are sub-divided into small groups and each selects a chairman. The proceedings of each are recorded. This gives an opportunity to make to lead the discussion and practise leadership roles. This technique may not be applicable in training local leaders, but is, in general, a very useful method of training.

*Giving Responsibility to Local Leaders*—Giving everyone a job through which self-confidence may be attained by achievement in activities useful to the group is an essential development of leadership.

One basic conclusion that emerges is that, if the extension workers are to extend educational programmes to reach more people and if the programmes are to achieve their objectives, they must exercise to the fullest extent the leadership role and increase the effectiveness in the development of leadership and group activity. Used in the right way, in the right situation, with the right subject and with the right group, they can be powerful in the promotion of training.

### *Adoption Process*

Adoption is not a sudden event, a gradual process. There are several well-known schemes for explaning the adoption process; i.e., awareness, interest, evaluation, trial and adoption, etc.

The Stages of Adoption Process:

*Awareness*—At this stage the individual is exposed to an idea but lacks detailed information about it. This is somewhat like seeing something without attaching meaning to it.

*Interest*—An individual at this stage is motivated to find out more about the new idea. He seeks more information which will help him to relate the new idea to the past experiences and other practices he has used. He wants to know what it is, how it works and what its potential may be.

*Evaluation*—Here the individual is concerned with mentally applying the idea to his present or predicted situation. He goes through a sort of mental assessment of the new edeas. An individual considers the relative advantages of the new practice over other alternatives.

*Trial*—If the mental trial is favourable, the individual will try to apply the new idea to a specific situation. He will then seek specific information regarding the technique and method of applying the new ideas. Most of the people will not adopt a change without trying it out first on a small scale.

*Adoption*—If the individual is satisfied with the trial, he decides to use the new practice, and thus adopts the innovations.

Another popular adoption process involves knowledge, persuasion, decision and confirmation.

These 4 stages have been elaborated by Rogers and Shoemaker as follows:

*Knowledge*—When the individuals learn that there are new inventions or innovations and they adopt to these they gain new knowledge.

*Persuasion*—When the individual forms a favourable or unfavourable opinion of the innovation.

*Decision*—When the individual engages in activities which lead to a choice between adoption and rejection.

Confirmation—When the individual makes a final decision to accept or abandon the innovation.

It is well known that some people are more innovative than others.

Adopters have been sub-divided into categories on the basis of the relative time they take to adopt innovations, such as early adopters, early majority, late majority and laggards. Innovativeness generally can be related to the following personal characterstics, background, social status affiliations, attitudes, etc.

programmes through extension education have three broad approaches, i.e. integrative, adaptive and project approach.

### *Integrative Approach*

Integrative approach emphasises on development and the co-ordination of technical services. This type of programme has the following characteristics :

(i) An agency, attached to a central planning office which is responsible for the programme.

(ii) There is cabinet level committee presided over by the Prime Minister or the President with the head of the Committee as the Secretary. This gives policy guidance and leadership to the programme.

(iii) There is a developmental committee at State level, district level. It has also representatives from local legislatives and private welfare organisations.

(iv) Workers views will be used to provide a link between villagers and the Government's technical services.

(v) Grant-in-Aid and other inducements are provided to channelise efforts to establish goals.

### *Adaptive Approach*

Adaptive approach lays emphasis on community organisation and self-help and involves little change in administrative organisation of government. It is designed primarily to stimulate self-help and to attract support of the technical departments. These are called 'adaptive' because they can be attached to almost any department and adapted to prevailing administrative organisation.

### *Project Approach*

This is a multi-functional approach, but limited to geographical scope of certain parts of the country. The structures of these types are such that they cannot be extended on a nation wide basis without interfering with the operations of other Government agencies.

## Uniqueness of the Extension Programme in India

India's extension programme covers the total development of community; it combines all the activities related to the promotion of the all-sided development of village communities including political, social, cultural and moral improvement, which is being called as a unique programme.

## Objectives of Extension Education

### *Broad Objectives*

The programme aims at the rapid increase of food and agricultural production, the promotion of education, improvement in health, introduction of new skills and occupations, so that the programme, as a whole, can raise the rural community to a higher level of economic organisation and arouse enthusiasm for new knowledge and improved ways of living. By this, the three most important factors which affect the country's economy, i.e., hunger, disease and ignorance, would be tackled through coordinated and planned ways. Its general objective is to secure the fullest development of natural and human resources.

In the words of C.C.Hearne, the objective behind the extension programme in India is "to raise the standard of living of the village population, and the right use of land, water and livestock".

### *Specific Objectives*

The following are the specific objectives of extension education.

1. To change the outlook of the people. Unless the people develop rising expectations for a higher level of living, there can be no motivation for the people to provide the required leadership and to assure that village development will become a continuous people's programme.

2. Development of responsive village leadership and of village organisations and institutions.

3. To develop village people to become self-reliant responsible citizens, capable and willing to participate effectively with knowledge and understanding to the Nation.

4. Continued emphasis is focused on improving and modernising agricultural practices and methods essential for increased agricultural production.

5. Improvement of existing, and organising the new, cottage industries towards increasing employment and income.

# 10

# EXTENSION EDUCATION AND DEVELOPMENT EDUCATION

## Overview

A dynamic and flexible type of education is one which serves the people wherever they are and whatever they are. Education assists in the development of the individual as well as the categories of the constituents of society.

'Development' is an exclusive term. It includes all the efforts taken towards the advancement of the interests of the community. It denotes and growth and development of a community. Hobhouse defines 'Social Development' as 'the overall movement towards greater efficiency and complexity but with the recognition of the concomitant problems'.

With this understanding about 'Development' let us now discuss the role, extension has to play towards the development of the community.

## Extension Education and Development

Extension education aims at improving the quality of the human being as a member of the community and to improve his/her knowledge and skill as a crop grower, dairy-man, home-maker, artisan, health, women and child welfare worker, non-formal and adult education organiser, etc. In general, the development

6. Need of food, clothing, shelter, recreation health and religion are crystalised within the family and the motivation for their achievement comes from within the family.

7. To upgrade the social status of the village teacher and to enable her/him to participate in the development programme.

***Steps in Organising Development Programmes***

To make the development programmes run smoothly and progress well, the following steps are suggested.

***Establishing Rapport in the Community***

Rapport is a condition of mental responsiveness between the extension worker and the learner with whom the work is done, in a way that both respond spontaneously to each other. The extension worker should be able to create confidence among the community. This requires the knowledge of the group, knowledge of the dynamics of planned change and the ways of motivating people.

***Appraising the Situation, Identifying the Problems and Needs***

For any programme of development a study of the present situation of the people, their problems and needs is necessary. The people should say what their felt needs are and what should be the priority among the various problems to be solved. The needs of the people constitute the core around which a successful development programme can be built.

***Planning the programme***

Planning is the formation of major economic decisions what and how much to produce, how, when and where to be produced and to whom it is to be allocated by the conscious decision of an accepted authority on the basis of a comprehensive survey of the economic system as a whole. The four major elements of planning are:

A plan for involving local people in the planning process, procedure in programme planning, the programme—the product of planning, and the annual plan of work.

***Selecting Initial and Long-Range Projects***

Short-term planning includes immediate problems—economic

and social, which need to receive immediate attention of the planners. It mainly takes the shape of partial planning, emergency planning or accidental planning. Long-term planning concentrates on basic problems facing the community all over the country.

### *Securing People's Participation*

Decision about the objectives of the programme is usually best when made both by the officials and the community or their representatives. This involvement or participation can be obtained possibly through some organised efforts or approaches. Organising the village people into farmers' organisations, youth clubs or women's associations, etc. makes the people get involved in programme planning and execution.

### *Developing Effective Communication Channels*

Communication is a conscious attempt to share information ideas, attitudes etc. It is the act of getting a sender of information tuned to the receiver. Here, the extension worker will be the sender of information and the people, the receivers. Good communication does not consist in just giving orders, but in creating understanding. It also does not consist of merely imparting knowledge, but helping people clearly understand the matter communicated. It is the act of saying the right things, at the right time, in the right way, to the right people on the right occassion, and obtaining right results in right direction.

The following communication channels make the people come closer to each other:

Transport facility-people come in contact with the outside world and become aware of the progressive ways of doing things; Mass media such as Radio, Newspapers, Films, Exhibitions, Puppet Shows, Television, Public meeting, etc.

### *Development and Use of Organisation Channels*

Organisation Channels here mean the organisation of male or female adults and youth according to their interests in occupational, recreational or interest groups. These may be farmers' organisations, women organisations or youth organisations. These voluntary organisations should be created by people and led by them.

### *Community Leadership*

In the development programmes, leaders are expected to initiate action which helps the community to adopt improved practices. While identifying leaders it is important to know what job is to be done, what characteristics and skills the job requires, where to find the person possessing the needed qualifications, what group will support or follow this person, which qualities can be improved by training and which may not be changed and how could the leader be induced to work for the community. Development aspects of extension in general there are three major aspects that are to be considered in Extension. Extension education centres around three units—the farmers or rural people or the clients.

## The extension workers and the extension for general purpose

### *Functions of Extension Education for Rural People*

Extension education imparts education leading to behavioural changes in the desired direction is a process of informing people, motivates people to adopt innovations, suggests alternative fields for the needs and resources of the people, involves active participation of the people, improves the decision making ability of the people, brings permanent improvement in the conditions of the people, helps to develop people's own programme, creates a congenial learning situation, and builds confidence through action and conviction.

Extension education for extension workers establishes job performance, helps in achieving team-spirit, assists in making workers organisation minded, trains the personnel as an in-built and continuous process and develops the morale of the workers and makes them highly professional in the above roles. Extension education for general purposes develops, strengthens and organises the groups, institutions and people to achieve their objectives, develops leadership in local and professional situations, acquaints the planners, policy makers and administrator. With local conditions and the latest technologies suited to it, provides sufficient data for developing plans and for coordination of activities, and gives direction and a package of educational practices for adoption and diffusion and also provides a communication media mix for innovations and evaluations.

Investment in education is necessarily long-term and begin to yield results after a generation and in some cases, even after a longer period. Developing countries, however, are pressed greatly for time; and hence an important issue is how to plan educational programmes which can yield quicker and almost immediate results. If such programmes can be identified and implemented, the developing countries will get a much better and quicker return for their investments in education and will stand more to benefit. Several programmes of this type can be suggested in extension education.

## Extension Education in Different Disciplines

### *Agriculture Extension*

This is concerned with agricultural Extension-assisting farmers to bring about continuous improvement in their physical, economic and social well-being through their individual co-operative efforts. It makes available to the farming community the scientific and other factual information, the training and guidance for the solution of the problems in agriculture including animal husbandary, gardening agricultural, engineering, etc.

Through agriculture extension the technical know-how of science in agriculture, Home making, etc. is carried to and include in the practices of farmers, home makers, animal breeders, etc. Extension education is education both formal and informal aiming at assisting people to bring about continuous improvement in their physical, economic, and social well-being through their individual and cooperative effort. Extension education is a two-way process whereby the problems of the client system are brought by the change agents like Agricultural Universities, Research Stations, Home Science Colleges, Veterinary Colleges, Medical Colleges, Adult Education Departments, NSS Units, etc., and the results are taken back to the client system in an acceptable form.

Singh M.P. (1966) says that there can be no one pattern of organisation for agricultural extension work. Each country has to develop its extension organisation according to its own social, cultural and economic conditions at a given stage in its development. He suggests the following measures to bring about agriculture extension programme.

1. Extension work can be most effective only when it is entirely educational in nature and free from regulatory and other government responsibilities.
2. As development proceeds more specialisation at the field level may be feasible and desirable. Where agriculture is diversified, a generalist extension officer who can look at the farm operation as a whole is needed at the field level.
3. The successful work of the generalists at the field level depends upon their being supported by specialists at the next higher levels of administration. As agriculture progresses, both the necessity of providing specialists at lower administrative levels will increase.
4. Efforts should be made to keep extension and research closely related to each other. This can be achieved by setting up an institutional channel and employment of subject matter specialists in the extension service and periodic contacts between research and extension staff through meetings, conferences, field trips, etc.
5. Extension work must be directed towards the family as a whole—men, women and children work together.
6. In the interest of providing maximum effective service within the limited resources, there is an urgent need for effective coordination of all the agencies serving rural people.

Extension services have to make available to people scientific and functional information in a manner that can be used by them to solve the problems of agriculture, home making and any problem in the community. And this involves getting the new knowledge from a source-usually. Agricultural Research situations, interpreting the knowledge so that people can understand it and transmitting the interpreted information, in an effective manner, to the people who will use it.

An extension organisation, in order to perform its functions effectively, must keep these considerations in view. A provision must be made in the organisational set-up for flow of useful information from the stations to the farmers and of farm problems back to the research station, production of teaching aids for use in extension work which involves setting up of an agricultural information cell within the extension division of the Ministry, a capable and trained extension staff who can transmit the useful information to the farmers and assist them to organise farming as a "business" and in order to facilitate this movement of information back and forth, the number of levels of extension administration should be kept as small as possible.

Because of the shortage of extension workers and lack of other resources in a number of developing countries, "there is an increasing tendency to concentrate them in limited areas, e.g., on specific development projects or areas which have greater potential for rapid agricultural development, rather than spread thinly over the entire country.

### *Culture*

Culture is the continuously changing pattern of learned behaviour and the products including attitudes, values, knowledge and material objects which are shared by and transmitted among members of society. The culture of the people of a community or society is dynamic. It continuously changes because of internal as well as external forces or stimuli. Development work aims at bringing a change in the culture of the rural people in a country. It is a planned programme for the promotion of cultural change among the rural people towards desired goals. Certain cultural factors that affect developmental work are being discussed as under:

### *Institutions*

The social institutions like government, family, religion panchayat, the educational system and the economic system are developed and promoted by the village people in their interaction with one another. These institutions also influence the culture of the people.

*Government.* In India, Panchayat is an institution which controls and direct people's affairs at village level. The extension worker must strengthen local confidence in it and channelise activities through Panchayats, at the time of elections he must make people think carefully about the selection of candidates.

This awareness has to be created among the people to strengthen the democracy and the local government.

*Family.* In a family, different members have different roles of behaviour and action. Activities like child-rearing, cooking, home management etc., can be changed through extension work with women. Agricultural development is possible through male heads of the family as well as women.

*Religion.* There are certain practices or things that are prohibited in certain religions and they follow certain practices. The extension worker must study the existing situations and use his knowledge to promote the desired change. For example, festivals like Deepavali, Christmas, Independence day, etc., can be used to provide opportunities for the promotion of home decoration, cleanliness, etc.

*Education.* The village school can be an effective channel for rural an development. The contents of education in village school should gear to village occupations. Projects in kitchen gardens, home garden, etc., can be introduced and promoted. Education can also change the life pattern of the people in the community. The extension worker can establish a close link between school and community to bring about change both in school and the community.

*Economic System.* Every society organises its relationships into a pattern that forms the physical means of livelihood. This pattern meets the economic needs. This includes the land tenure system as property and the occupational pattern. The extension worker must develop from this knowledge, the strategies to promote the economic status of the society. He/she could work through various agencies to provide employment to people.

### *Groups*

A group is defined as two or more people in reciprocal communication. The groups have common as well as divergent interest. The extension worker should understand the groups to gain rapport in disseminating information. He should plan the strategy in accordance with the influence of these groups.

### *Organisations*

Organisations are formalised groups, systematically arranged units of people with the object of achieving some common goal in which the role of each person is specifically prescribed.

***Patterns of Influence***

This means the leadership structure of power structure of the village. This is linked to an invisible network connecting an influencing village life in its various aspects. The extension worker must be able to identify villages who could play the role of a leader effectively.

***Value System***

A society places different values on the various items which forms part of village life and the differing values go together to form the value system. Some examples of these factors are truthfulness, honesty, caste, wealth and economic position, sincerity in work, etc.

***Media of Communication***

These are the means by which information or knowledge is passed from one group to another. This may be through gossip groups, play groups or through leaders. These changes can be made known to one another through channels like newspaper, radio, government officials, melas, etc.

## Role of Extension Worker

A professional extension worker is a guide, an enabler, an expert and a therapist.

***Role as a Guide***

In the capacity of a guide, the extension worker is required to help the community to find the means of achieving its goals, take initiative in working with people, be objective about conditions in the community, associate or identify himself with the whole community and not with any provide group, provide information on different ways of doing things and should never recommend a particular course of action and she/he should only assist the villagers in making decisions and show them the responsibility of performing the right action.

***Extension Worker as an Enabler***

1. The role of the extension worker as an enabler to facilitate

and accelerate the development process includes focussing discontent about community conditions.

2. The extension worker should listen patiently to the problem, encourage verbalisation by interrogation and help them to decide and attain a plan of action.
3. Encouraging organisation—the task of an extension worker is to initiate and faciiitate the process by which the discontent of the people is identified. He should make group come together, rank their discontent and organise to deal with their discontent. The extension worker should provide judgement on the problem.
4. Nourishing good interpersonal relations—the extension worker needs to be warm, friendly and sensitive to the deeper feelings of the people.
5. Emphasising common objectives—the extension worker should consistently work at facilitating the development of community through its leaders to realise its potentialities and strength in co-operative work.

### *Extension Worker as an Expert*

In the capacity of an expert, the extension worker should provide data and direct advice in a number of areas about which he may speak with authority. He must provide research data, technical experience, resource materials and advise on methods which the villagers may need and require in its operation.

### *Extension Worker as a Therapist*

It implies diagnosis and treatment of the community as a whole. This treatment should be carried through leaders of groups. The areas in which this treatment is required are taboos, ideas, traditional attitudes which create tension and separate the community. He should be able to recognise these evils and provide effective treatment.

## Home Science Extension

Preparing young girls for their future home making responsibilities has been the function of the mother and the grandmother in the past. But now this concept has undergone a considerable change. Today a nuclear family system and the young house-wife has to bear a lot of responsibilities. She is faced with the problem of selecting the right food, fabrics, equipment, housekeeping methods, child-rearing methods etc. from the large variety which the modern advances of science and technology and means of communication have rendered available to her. Home science extension education aims at educating the individual for family living, improving the services and goods used by families, conducting research to discover the changing needs of individuals and families and the means of satisfying these needs, and furthering community, national and world conditions favourable to family living.

### *Role of Home Science Extension in Rural Development*

While developing home science extension programme the extension worker has two responsibilities—to guide his/her clients in satisfying their felt needs and to contribute through the clients, in achieving the national goals.

In the process of programme planning the extension worker must help his/her clients in developing an awareness of the problems of the community and the nation. Some of the present day problems which could be included within the scope of creating awareness through home science extension are as follows :

Food and water storage, and preservation, poor health and nutrition, environmental pollution, illiteracy, over-population, poverty and lack of understanding and/or practice of democracy etc.

Home science extension has a definite role to play in assisting the rural home makers to contribute in solving many of these problems, as they perform their routine functions.

Home science extension work can result in a raised standard of living for the rural families, and a more satisfying and dignified life for them. This in turn inspires them to increase farm production. It is through home science extension the farm products any new food products, clothes and house hold equipment get popularised and accepted. This is one of the reasons for establishing home science things in the Agricultural Universities.

# 11

# EVALUATION THE EXTENSION IN EDUCATION

Evaluation is defined as the process of determining the extent to which the objectives have been attained. It is a continuous and comprehensive process which takes place at any place where a programme is carried out, whether school or outside in the field. In education it is designed to determine the effectiveness of instruction in respect of an individual learner or a group of learners taking into account the objectives and the changes taking place.

Evaluation covers a wider purpose than testing. Testing only aims at knowing the achievements of a student in a particular subject during a specified period and helps improve the curriculum, teaching strategies and process of evaluation. It is a dynamic procedure changing according to the needs and purposes. Evaluation helps us set goals and tasks which are higher than what we aspired for earlier programmes.

So, evaluation either in the classroom or in the field aims at improving the whole educational process and it is an integral part of all teaching and learning process.

## Objectives of Evaluation

1. It helps in testing the genuineness of objectives and helps in their modification.
2. It helps in judging the effectiveness of the methods of teaching in terms of the objectives of teaching.
3. It helps us identify the needs for concentrated effort.

4. It has a value in creating public confidence by giving rational facts.
5. It shows use whether the tools of teaching and the approaches followed in field work can be more wisely chosen.
6. It helps us define our objectives clearly before teaching and taking a project.
7. It helps in the improvement or modification of the evaluation tools and techniques which should not be static but should change from time to time.

## Purposes of Educational Evaluation

A comprehensive scheme of educational evaluation serves a number of purposes that ultimately contributes to the irnprovement of the instructional goals, strategies, curriculum, textbooks and attainment.

### *Prof. N.M. Downie Lists the Following as Purposes of Evaluation*

1. To provide information for grading, reporting to parents and promoting students.
2. To evaluate the effectiveness of a single teaching method or to appraise the relative worth of several methods.
3. To motivate the students, for learning and application of what is learnt.
4. To select the students for higher education.
5. To evaluate the entire educational institution and to show how various aspects could be improved.
6. To measure learner's knowledge of facts, principles, definitions, laws, experiments, etc.
7. To reveal to the teacher what learners have learnt—a feedback.
8. To show learners what they have learnt as the feedback to the learner.
9. To make comparisons among learners or among teachers or among institutions.
10. To encourage learning and by promoting healthy competition among learners.

11. To identify the aptitude of the learners for the extension work and to work with the community.
12. To identify the skills of the students for the required jole.
13. To certify the real level of the candidate for employment in suitable jobs after the completion of the school education.
14. To collect information for effective educational and vocational counselling.

## Types of Evaluation

Evaluation can be classified into the following seven types :

### *Diagnostic Evaluation*

Diagnostic type of evaluation is usually done in the beginning of the teaching—learning process in order to find out the specific weaknesses and strengths and aptitude of an individual or a class. This helps design the courses and activities according to the capabilities and aptitude of the learner to help him/her overcome his/her deficiencies in knowledge, skills and abilities.

### *Formative Evaluation*

Formative evaluation is concerned with making decisions relating to forming or development of students as well as of the courses. It provides feedback at appropriate stages of the teaching—learning process which helps in making changes in the curriculum, teaching strategies and the learning environment. Formative evaluation is done during the process of teaching–learning with the following main purposes.

(a) To monitor student learning for the purpose of providing individualised instruction, feedback and guidance.

(b) To evaluate teaching effectiveness and the strategies, approaches followed.

(c) To evaluate courses and curricula, with the purpose of modification and updating.

(d) To evaluate the teaching and learning environment with a view to improving it.

(e) To evaluate the attainment of the goals of the course or project.

### *Summative Evaluation*

Summative evaluation is concerned with making judgments about a finished product or process or a completed course of study. Terminal examinations whether internal or external are a good example of summative evaluation, but summative evaluation needs not necessarily be terminal. Cumulative assessments where they are undertaken solely for the purposes of selection, promotion, prediction, recording and such other administrative purposes, should also be considered as a series of summative evaluation.

### *Informal Type of Evaluation*

Formal evaluation involves planning and use of tools of evaluation like tests, questionnaire, score card, rating scale, etc.

Informal evaluation can be done as and when the programme is going on and need not be rigid. This type needs not employ the tools like tests, questionnaire, observation, schedule, etc.

### *Concurrent, Periodic and Phasic Evaluation*

Concurrent evaluation is done when the programme is going on to assess mainly the process.

Periodic evaluation is done after a certain period, say two or three months or even after a year, to see its progress and attainment.

Phasic evaluation is done after implementing a particular phase of the programme.

### *Internal, External and Self-Evaluation*

Internal evaluation means appraisal of a programme of action by members of the same organization. For example, a professor evaluating extension and community social service programmes conducted by him/her for his/her students. This is a continuous procedure as the teacher is also part of the programme.

External evaluation is conducted by individuals or groups outside the organization. For example evaluation of the performance of students of one institution by staff of another institution. Or an expert evaluating either progress or completion of a project.

Self-evaluation denotes the self criticism or appraisal or progress by the individual involved in the action himself/herself.

Self-evaluation is simply a process of continuously and honestly asking one self such questions as how well am I succeeding in doing the job etc. For example an extension worker asking him/herself how well he/she succeeded in each village contact, demonstration, discussion meeting, etc.

***Qualitative and Quantitative Evaluation***

Evaluation is also classified as quantitative and qualitative. Whenever the emphasis is on 'how much' or 'how many' aspects, the appraisal is quantitative; wherever it is on the manner or method of movement toward the goal is qualitative.

Qualitative and quantative evaluation is done in programmes like introducing smokeless *chulahs* to the villages, having improved toilets, etc. Where we evaluate the number of adopters of the schemes is quantative. When we evaluate the steps followed in the programme whether we have made all the people aware of the uses of, improved toilets and smokeless *chulah*, then we undertake qualitative evaluation.

## Evaluation Procedures

Evaluation is a continuous process and consists of the following stages :

1. Formulating and selecting worthwhile objectives of teaching and learning and the field work.
2. Clarifying and defining the objectives in terms of expected learning outcomes or behavioural changes in learners and adopters.
3. Developing appropriate learning experiences or activities.
4. Devising and adopting suitable assessment procedures to collect adequate and trustworthy evidences about the learner's achievement and the achievement of the objectives of the project.
5. Evaluating the outcomes on the basis of the evidences collected and modifying the necessary aspects of the entire system.

For an evaluation procedure to be completed, it must pass through the following three well-defined steps:

***Step 1***

Formulating objectives of teaching and translating them in terms of desired changes to be brought in the learner and in the field.

***Step 2***

Determining and providing learning experiences appropriate to the objectives of the project or the course.

***Step 3***

Preparing tools of evaluation to measure or assess the extent to which contemplated learning experiences and the changes have actually taken place in the learner and the changes in the field.

## Components of Extension and Evaluation

Knowledge gained in the classroom is to be tested in the field for its applicability. The extension worker, therefore, requires the following: (a) Knowledge of the subject, procedures. (b) Aptitude for field work. (c) Ability to implement the procedures. (d) Ability to observe the events and facts. (e) Ability to record the observed events and facts accurately. (f) Ability to handle the data. (g) Ability to interpret the data. (h) Ability to draw conclusion. (i) Ability to device alternate procedures and (j) Ability to write report.

Another set of skills needed for and extension worker are Social skills like (a) Co-operativeness, (b) Team spirit, (c) Leadership, (d) Interest in others (individual and groups), (e) Good manners, (f) Good personal and social relationships, (g) Ability to get along with others, (h) Ability to identify oneself with, participate in and contribute to social activities and purposes.

The extension worker should possess personal traits such as (a) motivation, (b) independence, (c) initiative, (d) self-discipline, (e) responsibility, (f) drive, (g) sociability, (h) leadership, (i) self-confidence, (j) emotional maturity, (k) balance, (l) integrity, (m) punctuality, (n) neatness, (o) clean-liness, (p) orderliness, (q) reasonable speed in everything, (r) hard work, (s) regularity and originality.

Extension worker should have communication skills like receiving and orally communicating ability in dialogue and discussion and in written form, of report-writing and drawing. While speaking proper pronunciation, accent, intnation, modulation and control of voice should be observed. In writing, content, formations, spacing, neatness, legibility, etc. should be given emphasis.

When the students go to the fields or laboratory areas for extension work, they should possess the knowledge required in the specific area of extension, pay attention to or observe related phenomena occurring in the environment, join, assist, co-operate and participate in the activities, visit places of interest, initiate and invite others for discussion, identify and solve challenging problems and never leave the problems unsolved. The extension worker should have healthy, positive and scientific attitude should seek fresh clues, evidences to solve problems, accept opinions of others on convincing proof, consider new interpretation, arguments, evidence, possibilities and ideas with an open heart, report honestly in clear and precise terms what has been observed, accept errors in opinions without hesitation, suspend any judgment till adequate evidence is available and arrive at conclusions on the basis of objective measurements and logical proofs.

## Evaluation Procedure

How to evaluate all these traits of an extension worker or a student involved in extension activities will be a very big question to those who have to evaluate. It could be done best when it is a continuous, periodic and internal assessment. This means that assessment is done in relation to certain abilities, competences and skills periodically and continuously. This is internal because it is to be done by the teacher who teaches or guide the subject in the institute and not an external examiner. The knowledge, objectives, attitude, aptitude and skills or competence needed for the particular task should be clearly spelt out.

Internal assessment in addition to providing a grade of the performance in the field and product of an individual as and when the process is on, should also generate information and provide feedback to improve further both teaching and learning procedures.

The internal assessment marks should be made open to the learner. The learner should have a correct opinion about his/her own performance from the evaluator so that his/her performance could be improved.

Along with this internal assessment and providing a grade for it, we could also have an external terminal evaluation at the end of the programme or course and the marks or grades could be shown separately in the mark or grade-sheet as both these assessments assess different aspects. Percentage of allotment of marks for internal and external may be 50-50. If we combine both internal and external marks for final grading there may be a tendency to boost up the internal marks of their students, in some cases it may be reversed, score less in internal and score more in external. Grading can be done and shown separately where there is need for an external assessment, rather than combining both for awarding a final grade or class.

## Weightage for Performance, Continuous Internal Assessment

We may allot the marks for various components as detailed below:

| | |
|---|---|
| (a) Aptitude for community work | - 20 marks |
| (b) Regularity | - 10 " |
| (c) Human relationship | - 20 " |
| (d) Execution of project | - 20 " |
| (e) Reporting | - 30 " |
| Total | 100 marks. |

Marks could also be awarded as shown:

10+ - Outstanding ability
8-10 - Above average
5-7 - Average ability
1-4 - Below average
0 - No ability

We could also have another procedure of evaluating or grading on the basis of criteria fixed:

| | |
|---|---|
| 4 – Outstanding | – A |
| 3 – Above average | – B+ |
| 2 – Average | – B |
| 1 – Below average | – C |
| 0 – Not satisfactory | – D or F |

A format for evaluating the extension work has been given (Table 11.1). It is only a suggestive format. The evaluator can formulate or prepare his/her own format depending on the project, objectives of evaluation, availability of time, resources, etc.

The evaluation format could be project specific.

**Table 11.1 : Evaluation of Extension Work : A Format**

| *Major categories* | *Sub sections of each category of assessment* |
|---|---|
| 1. Selection of the theme for the | Relevance of the theme selected; needs; objectives; attainability of the objectives originality; innovation; knowledge about the theme/problems. |
| 2. Planning | Formulating objectives; design of the project; approach; preparation of tools; alternate plan. |
| 3. Execution | Approach to task; understanding the local conditions–people: skill of communication, willingness to learn from others; willingness to correct errors if any; active participation; organising capacity; initiativeness; ability to integrate with other organisations. |
| 4. Ability to handle the tools and equipment | Use of A.V. equipment; choice of aids; skill of using; overcoming difficulties; thoroughness; accuracy; ability prepare audio-visual aids. |
| 5. Recording | Proper observation of details; accuracy in recording; appropriateness and usability of data recorded; reducing and correcting. |
| 6. Interpretation of data | Selection of appropriate tool for calculation; translation of data into meaningful action plan, ability to interpret and replan for the future; originality. |
| 7. Report-writing | Knowledge and skill of writing the observed facts; ability of presenting in a readable form; knowledge of the similar studies to interpret and write the present report. |
| 8. Aptitude | Interest in the work undertaken; sincerity; punctuality; positive approach to the problems and the people; tolerance; co-operative; adjustable and supportive; neutral. |
| 9. Overall Assessment compeletish | On the basis of all the criteria cited above this could be assessed and graded from A to F or marks could be awarded. |

This format is just suggestive. The one who evaluates the performance of students' work is free to modify and change for awarding the grade or marks.

# 12

# FUTURE OF EXTENSION IN EDUCATION

## Scenario in the Next Millenium

Any change will reflect the past at least two decades of the previous century. Shall we say that the 21st century will reflect the last two decades of 20th century? Becuase nothing can emerge from a vacuum. All what we have today will certainly be reflected in the next scenario of the 21st century at least for about a decade, as present generation is going to handover the knowledge to the next generation to generate new knowledge. Thus this continuity will be seen in the next decade, say upto 2010, till the new knowledge and skills emerge and replace the past.

Human resource is the best resource of a society. Experience show that the qualitative development of a society is directly proportional to the qualitative as well as quantitative development of the human resources of any society.

"Man is a citizen of the world, a member of the vast commonwealth of nature" and to the interest of this great community, he ought, at all times, to be willing that "his own little interest should be sacrificed".

***(Adam Smith–Economist)***

Planned development, management and utilization of human resources can give maximum impetus to the progress of a society.

The indicators of development and the parameters of growth and development are changing. However, the condition of health, elementary education, women's status, income generation, skill development, employment, etc. are the important indicators of measuring the social progress of human race, rather than the simple change in per capita income.

Education is to be decentralised. All the agencies working in rural areas like Panchayat Raj institutions, Gramasabhas, Voluntary organisations, Educational institutions, Co-operaties, Government departments and the enlightened citizens should actively participate in educational activities. This implies that education cannot be restricted to the four walls of classrooms. Education should relate itself to the needs of the people, locale specific, which indicates that the curriculum cannot be uniform throughout the country.

Curriculum is to be framed according to the requirements and the culture of the society. This will demand the educationists to go out to the community and stretch their hands to find out the needs of the people and plan the education accordingly, instead of sitting away from the community and give a uniform curriculum to be followed throughout the country.

People must have inclination towards the right to improve their standard of living and to build their capacity. Educational institutions should create a right environment to empower the people. This is possible only when the educational institutions make extension as an essential component of their system.

Dr. Madhuri R. Shah, chair person of University Grants Commission once said "the University system of the future would thus be three–dimensional. The third dimension besides the age old objectives of teaching and research which has to be added is of 'extension'. Extension has generally come to be accepted as the third arm of the University system". A graduate of tomorrow should, therefore, be judged or evaluated for what she/he has learnt in the classroom as well as what has she/he has done to the society.

Economic growth and development of a country is determined by its human, physical and financial resources. Even an abudance of natural and physical resources, machinery and capital may go under utilized, unutilized or misused if human resource factors are not adequately managed. The changing environment at the global level indicates that we should martch towards a quality development and products. This requires a scientific bent of mind, temper and workforce. Education should therefore, to respond to these emerging challenges so as to field in future, the men and women of calibre and competence of international standard so that we could work for a better future.

## Towards a Changing World

Rapid technological development, industrial revolution, demographic transition, political development, economic revolution, cultural erosion, etc. have made social change an inevitable and a common phenomenon. All these changes will take us to a completely new and even alien world for which we must be ready. We should keep pace with the changing world by changing our attitude towards the educational system and the services provided, otherwise we will be pushed back. Education has to play a crucial role because it is through education human being can quickly learn how to control the rate of change in personal affairs as well as in society at large.

The system of education which gives under importance to more knowledge and information gathering will have to be changed to proceed towards total development. We need to understand the workforce and human resources needed in the job market in future and educate them accordingly. There should be a balance between supply and demand. For certain sectors we have surplus manpower, in some we have shortage of skilled manpower. This type of imbalance will lead to the problem of educated unemployment and underemployment.

The present system of education has narrowed down the scope of life of educated youths, making a large chunk of people useless and unproductive. Only on completion of their study they understand that they are unfit or misfit in this world. It is therefore, the responsibility of education to give them right direction for their future career and life.

## Extension to be an Organic Link

The courses in future will be redesigned to be relevant and significant not only to students but also to nation as a whole and help in bringing about social transformation and national development. Various courses offered in the educational system today have undertaken extension in a sporadic way. All the disciplines should be organically integrated within the framework of teaching, research and extension covering knowledge and community–based educational and service areas.

Education itself is going to face a severe shock or futuristic threat due to tremendous knowledge explosion, technological development and ever–increasing population. Knowledge explosion will make today's knowledge a mis-and inadequate information for the coming days. Advance mass-communication technology has a greater impact on the psycho-social life of the teachers as well as the learners. The future generation is going to be highly informed society.

Providing more knowledge will not satisfy them, rather it would be a frustrating experience to them. To face the future with confidence and certainty both teachers and the learners must be able to visualise the changing scenario get themselves ready to face it.

## Teachers' Role in Extension

The teachers' role would be very crucial as they have to direct the learners to face the new world and shape it accordingly. Teachers and others who would impart the new knowledge and develop skill to impart this to the community will be recruited and trained for the specific purpose. The survival of these personnels will depend on competitive performance. Produce and publish or perish would be the future recruitment policy. Changing social, economic, political scenario through out the globe show that there should be high flexibility, adaptability, capacity to usher dramatic changes with fine tuning would be the need of the 21st century.

But do the teachers realise their vital role as the change agents? Inspite of the in service programmes it seems to be difficult for the teachers to change their old habits and they are neither ready to accept the innovations nor to invent something to suit the future. It is felt that the present education has failed to sustain its impact on teachers. But they cannot stand aloof for long. Unless they change themselves and be prepared to accept a future with a differentiated curriculum and teaching learning strategy they may not be able to survive.

If we want to make any headway in revolutionising the whole system of education then we have to first infuse in our teachers the ideology of future consciousness through well–organised in-service-education programme for the teachers. We should also revamp the pre-service training of teachers to face the future, with confidence.

## Educational Institutions and Community

All educational institutions will have autonomy to frame their own curriculum, strategies of teaching learning and evaluation system. These will depend on the marketability and the consumer. Quality would be the main concern of education which would be of great use to the people-user friendly. Professionalism, teaching and learning and management is to be maintained. Use of educational technology and media would reduce the cost of education making education to be individualistic.

## Educational Institutions and Industries

Workspots should work together and be the way of life for mutural benefits in the interest and development of human resources and the nation.

Formal education system of today should help to break down privileges, eliminate exploitation and open opportunities for the advancement of weaker sections of the society. It should come out of its rigidity to make available education to all the sections of the society. It could no longer remain as an obstacle to attain the goal of quality education for all.

## Diversification of education-flexibility in classroom

Today's universities like factories turn out graduates who are hardly tested for their practical worth and social relevance. Education has to take place in documentation centres, clubs, meeting-seminar halls, leisure centres, and are to be self financing in nature no depend on the Government. There has to be a shift from scoring marks to all round development. Emphasis should be on liberal use of books and journals in the liberary, computers for creating, processing, storing and retrieving information. Audio-visual equipment, other software and integrated information technology (in IIT) will have to be used in classrooms. Education for sustainable development to be remodelled for self employment. The stress should be on application of knowledge with reference to the community need or education to be need-based.

Education should come out of the portals of schools, colleges and universities and be open to all through open learning or distance learning. This system of distance education will call for more people to participate in teaching learning process. Education can not be confined to mere theoretical framework. It should attract people of all types of potentialities. The high and low achievers should feel that they could also get equal opportunity for learning and to bring out their potentialities.

Extension education can play a crucial role in this system of distance education which would be need-based. Every learner should be able to recognise his/her interest, ability not only in getting educated but also in the career. If they find it difficult to recognise, it is the task of the teaching community to identify and provide guidance so that there will be no wastage and stagnation of human resources. Youths with social consciousness and commitment will take up extension as a powerful tool to have greater linkage between Government's plans and the targetted beneficiaries in the community.

There should be link and interaction between institutions and the industry or the field. As teaching and learning is a two-way process the teacher himself/herself should be a learner as well as part of teaching process. The faculty can be deputed to go and have first hand, on the spot and hands on experiences in the field or area. This will enable them to gain new knowledge on the subjects they teach. These experiences will help them know the actual problems faced in the field for them to modify their approaches and equip themselves to solve the problems.

This link will also ensure excellence in terms of attainment of national goals, quality education for all, women's participation in nation building activities by empowering them, ensuring income for the citizens to support their needs through a planned, intensive intervention programme by finding out the local needs and resources and protection of environment to remove starvation, oppression, exploitation and unemployment from the society.

Faculty interaction with the society will improve not only their teaching but also their research. Their researches then will become need-based. Problems of the society and their needs will be the basis for their research and their findings will be taken back to the community for application and feedback. On the whole the link between society and the educational institution will make education highly flexible and move towards academic excellence.

## Science and Extension in 21st Century

Discoveries and inventions in science and technology have changed the world and given new laws and theories about growth and development of the universe. Inventions and discoveries are not sudden. Science goes step by step and stage by stage. Scientific inventions of today go back to the early age. Science of today is not one man's idea or discovery by over night. Many have added bit by bit to a great structure of knowledge, i.e. science.

Scientific knowledge has changed the structure of the society and the quality of life. The impact of science is seen in every walk of life of people. The knowledge explosion and easy spreading of message in 21st century will have a great impact on the social, economic and cultural scenario. There will be universalisation of science education every where and it will be reflected in the attitude and activities of people. There will be a greater demand from the society for its scientific applications in every day life. The educational institutions should be ready to respond to these demands in the next millennium by providing relevant and realistic knowledge to the learners.

The curriculum is to be restructured to suit the growing demands of the people. The community will provide the clues for curriculum construction and the educated mass should be able to transact on these needs and provide needed inputs. Science curriculum has to be need-based; researches in science will reflect these needs. Problems of the community will be researched and the solutions will have to be ploughed back to the community for their utility, which means science cannot remain as the symbol of the geneous in the portals of educational institutions.

The scientists will come out to the community to understand the needs and problems of people and take back to the class rooms for analysis and solutions. Learning and teaching of Science will be of two-way process. Outreach programmes or the extension programmes in science whether physical or bioscience will become integral part of science curriculum.

Instead, learning by-heart the concepts and theories in science, students will have to be exposed to the application of these in life situations for which they will have to go out to the community. Demonstrate what they have learnt in the class room, in the homes and farms and see its applicability and usability. They may have to reject what is not suitable and cannot be applied. Study of physics, chemistry, botany and zoology should have relevance to the life outside so that, when it is demanded this knowledge could be put to use.

Students should be taught as to how the scientific concepts be disseminated for effective use. Modern techniques of communication, use of mass media and strategies of extension will have to form part of curriculum transaction at all levels. Achievement of students will not be measured merely on the basis of the papers they write but also what they do to the community.

## Environmental Awareness through Extension

Nature's precious resources are getting scarce because of indiscriminate and unplanned acts of human race. Rapid industrialisation, mechanisation of human life and scientific inventions have made human life comfortable, but at the same tiem these have created new problems of air pollution, water pollution, noise pollution and soil pollution and created many new diseases. In themad race of development we have forgotten to take care of side effects of environment and its pollutions. We must move towards a green millennium.

The need of the hour and the future is to prepare suitable strategies of environmental education for saving the environment and future generation. Environmental education includes study of environment and its dynamics; environmental degradation and its various forms and factors degrading environment and its impact on man's life. These concepts are to be taken directly to the community, than merely teaching in educational institutions as a subject of study for examination and award of a degree or certificate.

It is only through extension services we could reach the community which is mainly responsible for the degradation and excess use of the natural resources. Through street plays, exhibitions and other electronic media we should make the mass learn the need for protecting and preserving the nature for future.

In every discipline of study the environmental concepts could be integrated and all the students and the faculty should realise their responsibility in taking this message of "preserve the nature for a better future" to the community. So, the future which is uncertain should give importance to environment education through extension programme. Unless we preserve the nature the future will be bleak. Forests are to be preserved. It will be the responsibility of every individual to ensure that trees are planted and forests are protected, as they are the resources of the community and the life of the generation.

## Mass Media in Extension

Modern, formal education become a reality for the common man with the adoption of the most important mass media, print, but it has been slow to adopt other media. Broadcasting media like radio and television are being used for support and enrichment of formal education but not replaced the teaching techniques followed.

The expansion of TV network has been phenomenal with the launching of INSAT/B in 1983 and followed by other satellite. This expansion has taken TV programmes to almost any location of the country.. Similarly other electronic media have come into existance in spreading the message to any part of the world. New knowledge and innovations could be taken quickly to any part without any difficulty. Extension worker in the next millennium should be ready to accept the mass media and use them in taking the new concepts and knowledge to the people.

When we use mass communication strategies for extension we should select them on the basis of their practiceability, feasibility, accessibility and affordability rather than highly sophisticated ones with high technicalities. Educational institutions should first of all ensure that the entire range of learning support facilities is available with them. The focus should be on providing skills development and competence promotion programmes to students who are on the threshold of higher education. This programme should aim at developing in them an understanding of the methods of communication, storage of information,

information retrieval, skills and oral communication skills. Students are to be made to realise their role in the learning programme where learning neither begins nor ends within the four walls of the classrooms. They should realise that real education commences only when they leave the portals of educational institutions and start serving the community. Every individual should have proficiency in preparing softwares for the mass media and operate the hardware.

## Link up Between Social Science Department with the Community

As the social sciences deal with different aspects of society, namely human behaviour, socio-psychological, economic, political, and cultural, the social scientists have sufficient expertise in understanding these different dimensions and therefore, they can easily notice and identify any problems in the society and their nature. They can also easily understand various schemes launched by the Governments and other agencies, especially to the downtrodden and the deprived sections of the society like the scheduled castes, tribals, widows, aged people, children, orphans and other needy people.

The faculty and the students should be able to take those welfare schemes of Government to the people concerned, through their extension work, instead of merely knowing these schemes. The community should become their laboratory to test what they learn in the classroom. They have to be the change agents of the society by understanding the feelings, and opinions of the common people by involving them both in planning and executing the schemes. They should follow the participatory approach to appraise the needs of people so that the people in the society is aware of their own requirements and others and the ways of satisfying them.

The social scientists should bring back the problems faced by them in the field to research them in the universities and take back the results of the research to the field. Thus the problems for the social science research have to come from the field as the result of the implementation of various schemes in the society than from the libraries.

## Role of Community in Extension

"One of the biggest mistakes we made when we gained independence was not to have overhauled thoroughly our educational system and structure. We are paying for it" said Mrs. Gandhi (1973). Yes it is true that we have not made the community to take up the responsibility of educating its people. There is need for educational institutions but the learning is not to be confined to the classrooms only. The individual is learning continuously from what is happening to him/her and around her/him from the people with whom the individual is interacting from the books and from the events of the world.

Only by learning from what happens in the society the individual could be socialised. As Swami Vivekananda has put it 'education is not what a person learns but what he becomes'. Life for a child, whether in a village or in a city should open out the windows to all the world's culture, heritage and knowledge. The learner should keep in touch with the fast changing world, if we want the learner to be useful to the society. It is not that the Government should spend money for the education of a few and they serve a few. We must produce more and more young people to serve the villages and their own places rather than flying away from their places and country. We see this brain drain especially in developing countries. The educated run away from their countries for a better position in some other countries wasting the money of their country spent on them.

We are producing many general graduates who are not trained for any specific job or skill, nor they have the adaptability or resourcefulness to make a place for themselves in society. Instead of making people self reliant, education is actually making them more dependent on government or on industry.

In 21st century it is the local community that would decide what will be the best form of education for their wards, plan the curriculum locally and execute it. It will then be more need-based and the educated will not become a misfit in the society and unemployable. Education will have a close contact with the realities and the problems of the society. The individual will have to learn to solve the problems of his community. This link between the educational institutions and the community will become inevitable. Educating its people will become the responsibility of the society.

So, the third dimension of education and the educational institutions will be community owned autonomous institutions. Extension will automatically become an important component of education system in the next millennium. Education will take place mostly outside the class rooms, according to the child's natural and human environments. Shall we say that the next millennium will move towards a 'Deschooled society', where the learning will take place outside the classrooms not within the four walls of the educational institutions.

# Index